I0638244

Lucas and the Time-Traveling Fog

The Revolution

Benjamin Vena

Lucas and the Time-Traveling Fog
The Revolution

First paperback edition 2025

Book design by Benjamin Vena
Cover artwork by Steven Vena

ISBN 979-8-3507-4525-2 (paperback)

Published by Lulu Publishing
www.benjaminvena.com

LUCAS AND THE TIME-TRAVELING FOG SERIES

LUCAS AND THE TIME-TRAVELING FOG
THE PARTY ANIMALS
UNFINISHED BUSINESS
A FIELD TRIP TO REMEMBER

To All of Our Fallen Heroes
You May Be Gone But Are Never Forgotten

Table of Contents

Chapter 1 - Hold The Line..1

Chapter 2 - Let's Talk...7

Chapter 3 - Keepsakes...17

Chapter 4 - The All-American Boy..25

Chapter 5 - Wake Up Call..39

Chapter 6 - Misfits...51

Chapter 7 - War...59

Chapter 8 - Good Samaritan..69

Chapter 9 - Close Encounter...79

Chapter 10 - Aftermath..91

Chapter 11 - Distraction...105

Chapter 12 - Renée...117

Chapter 13 - One Who Cried Wolf..131

Chapter 14 - Party Crashers..137

Chapter 15 - Mr. Damsel In Distress..145

Chapter 16 - From Beyond The Grave 153

Introduction

To those who know me, I'm sure you've heard plenty of my adventures through time thus far. If you don't, well hello my name is Lucas Robinson and here's a little refresher of what the fog has put me through. It all started in a small town in Hawkesville, Illinois where in the year 2019 when I was just starting out as a senior in high school, a Mysterious Green Fog appeared out of nowhere and brought me to the year 1959 where I lived the life of another highschool senior Gary Walter. Life wasn't easy but somehow I made it work. But as soon as I made some friends and a girlfriend, a highschool bully by the name of Henry Robinson came along and tried ruining my hard work. If the last name sounds familiar, that's my grandfather whom I never met in person until that fateful day where we ended up drag racing each other.

The true winner of that race was undetermined as the green fog came right when we were neck in neck and dragged me away into the life of a goody two-shoes college girl named Elizabeth Ross. Who just so happened to be the roommate of my...mother. Yeah, I know...awkward. I thought I was meant to be bringing my parents together as they had met in college but through trial and error, I learned that wasn't the case at all. Instead I was supposed to help Elizabeth Ross fall in love all that time.

When my "girl" fun was over, the Fog seemed to be done with me and put me back to the then present 2019. Everything changed after that…for starters your boy got a girlfriend by the name of Emily Stewart and that's when the whole world went nuts. Literally. This pandemic called Covid-19 took over and as a result my childhood and what normal life I thought I had ended on March 13th of 2020. During my isolation I got bored and became nostalgic. Now thanks to technology, I did some digging on the two people who I helped. I first did Gary Walter and was surprised to learn of his unfortunate fate. I was devastated beyond belief and begged the fog (if it has ears) to let me fix that mistake. Too bad I had to wait three boring years almost for it to finally happen. During that time I never once forgot what it was like living in Gary Walter or Elizabeth Ross' shoes.

Now when the mysterious time traveling green fog finally came back for me, I made a deal with the fog that I would be its helper for as long as it needs me just as long as it puts me back where I left and it worked. I was back in Gary Walter's body but it turned out that the fog put me back further than I expected. Thus leaving me stuck and having to play the long game. When the time eventually came to face destiny, I became the victor but it came at a cost. My adventure seemed to only get started as the fog then put me into the life of Benjamin Harper in the year 2002.

Which if you haven't already guessed is one year after I was born. My fun didn't stop there as I learned pretty quickly that I had to relive every adult´s worst nightmare and that is going to MIDDLE SCHOOL AGAIN! Specifically 8th grade where I had to save a friendship from ending before the class field trip to Washington DC was over. Once I saved the day as usual I found myself whisked away once again in another time period that seems to be farther away than 2002. I don´t know who I am or where I am but I do know that I landed on a college campus protesting the Vietnam War. Apparently I have a girlfriend as she just kissed my cheek and handed me an orange peace sign. So now that you are all caught up on my past escapades with the fog, let's see where we are going now.

Chapter 1

Hold The Line

Looks like my little backstory worked. You're here! Awesome! You're probably wondering two things; ONE where was I? and TWO who exactly is the girl who handed me the peace sign? Now judging by the bell bottom jeans, the tie dye shirt, a denim jacket with the same orange peace sign logo patch on my right arm that she had. I knew we were in a group together and most importantly realized that we are in a relationship as no random girl gives a guy a kiss on the cheek like that. Suddenly that same girl looked at me worried as I was feeling the left side of my face, and asked "Hey are you okay?" While still holding the sign she had just given me.

"I-I-I'm not really sure," I stammered

The young black woman chuckled to herself saying "I get that. It's overwhelming, isn't it? The sea of people surroundin us and all. Like those supporting our cause." As she glanced at the countless number of people around us "While others are giving

1

yuh the cold shoulder." gesturing to the dozen or so on-lookers facing us. She continued "But we can't stop now babe. We have to keep fighting. We have to keep pushing for change or else how will our soldiers ever come home!"

R–i–i–i–i–ght. Change. Got it loud and clear sergeant.

Just then someone from our group hollered "Oh no, it's the Pigs!"

Pigs? I don't see any pink critters running around here except...ohhh they must mean cops because oh boy here come a few now. Four I am assuming campus police officers in tan polo shirts and black baggy dress pants came with batons in full view as if that was some sort of threat. The ringleader of the four took one step forward to announce "Alright that's enough, you people must leave now or else I'll have no choice but have my men arrest every single one of yuh."

Someone from our group suddenly begins to shout "No. NO. We won't go!"

Then the crowd of protesters chant along with "my" girlfriend on repeat. Looks like things were about to turn ugly if it wasn't for the same cop who blew his whistle and shouts

"Who's the ringleader here?! Let me have a word with 'em." Suddenly I felt someone grab my one hand that was free and watched it rise and wave my arm high in the air for the whole world to see. I looked around and noticed that this was "my" girlfriend's doing as she proudly announced "We are." The crowd then roared like we were at a football game as one of our club members took our signs and gently pushed us forward to confront the officers. The crowd suddenly became quiet as the cops took us aside and one of them said in a hush tone "Can you do something to stop this racket?" My supposed "girlfriend" scoffed in disgust with that comment and asked "Can you stop the draft from happening and bring our men home?

The officer deadpanned to her and with a heavy sigh said "No."

"Then we won't leave!" She proudly proclaimed facing the crowd which began to rally with enthusiasm.

"Wait" I stammered. But was silenced by the echoing voices of the crowd. She then faced the officer and continued shouting

"And will never leave this here spot until—"

"That's enough!"

I angrily shouted. Silencing her in the middle of her sentence and the crowd that slowly started to rally behind her. Even the cops were startled. I turned to the officers and said mid whisper "Sorry about her fellas. As you can see she's a very...uh driven kind of person." I coughed awkwardly and added "Look I know that we are in our rights to have our little protest. So what's the real problem?"

The cop looked at me as if surprised that a person of my "looks" would know this sort of stuff and answered

"I'm aware, kid. I'm aware of your groups' rights. It's just that we had reports of your group becoming a little too violent see and—"

"Oh I see." My girlfriend rudely interrupts. "So when they do the same thing to us and we report it, you don't do a damn thing…but when they do it—"

"Babe!" I angrily interrupted and shouted. "I got this." Just then a black female with black wavy hair wearing the same uniform as us shouted "Yeah you tell'em Renée! You tell 'em!" Oh so that must be my girlfriend's name. Got it. Makes that so much easier than calling her babe all the time. But whoever that black woman with the wavy hair is, I gotta keep my eyes and ears on the lookout for her and her antics more often. Anyway, I then asked the officers "Will you excuse us for a minute?" They nodded so I pulled her away and reminded Renée by blatantly asking her "What are you doing? I'm trying not to get us arrested here. An arrest wouldn't look good…for our cause now would it?" She huffed and looked back at the officers and back at me twice before answering "Your right Eric. You're totally right. That wouldn't look good for the paper. Looks like we're gonna have to find anotha way." She then looked at the crowd who were anxiously waiting for her response.

But before she could say another word to "our" followers, whipped her head back at me and proclaimed "But our work here ain't over. We'll be back soon. Very soon." she then sighed and joked " I guess it's about time we have that talk with Marcus about his attitude sooner rather than later." We then told the officers that we would leave right away which they were happy with but warned us that if our followers did anything violent of any kind, they would be back and we would be to blame. I guess that must've triggered Renée as she gravitated to and shouted at "our" group "You heard the man let's go home." The crowd didn't buy it as I was chuckling at her expense. That's when I realized that all eyes were on me and all of them were patiently waiting for an answer. So I had to be the one to get the ball rolling to announce to all of them that "You heard her right folks. Let's get outta here but we'll be back here real soon. You'll see." The crowd upon hearing this cheered, murmured to themselves and finally dispersed. So I'm an Eric…huh. That's new.

Wonder what else I will find out while I am here?

Chapter 2

Let's Talk

Upon leaving campus heading to my car I believe, I felt my left hand had...had some sort of weight to it. Like I had jewelry on that hand. I looked at my fingers thoroughly, that's when I noticed that I had a brown leather watch on my wrist, a "Class of 1966" ring on one finger and on another had a ring but with no markings or letters, only a ruby in it that strangely gave off a green glow when I stared at it more. Suddenly I felt someone squeezing my free hand. A closer look on who it was is none other than Renée and when I looked at her hand, my heart stopped. I saw on her right hand a ring and not just any ring that she had but that of an engagement ring. It was gold and shined just like the bright sun that is out now. There was a time where I used to believe in coincidences but now I don't anymore. This is just another reason why. The only thought coursing through my head was *This can't be good.*

What I mean by that is Renée sounds like a sweet and caring woman, don't get me wrong and I am sure any guy would love to marry her. But I am not the one to do that. You see I am what you call "taken" and have a loving girl of my own back home waiting for me. But the thought of being stuck here and marrying someone is a risk I have no choice but to take and only thinking of my girlfriend Emily back home is slowing me down. The one thing besides Emily keeping me from lagging behind from the others is to find a mirror, any mirror because that look the cop gave me earlier still left a bad taste in my mouth.

Apparently it didn't take long for that idea to diminish as I was being led to a parking garage. While the other group of I don't know TWENTY FOUR other people got in their separate cars and trucks along the way. As for me and a few others, we kept on moving. I decided now was a good time to make a quick pit stop at one of the car mirrors that was parked along the way to our destination. One look at my new reflection and I froze. In the mirror, I saw that I was this muscular White man wearing a jean jacket and tie-dye shirt. Yes, you heard that right I was finally a man…a manly man once again! This time I had something I thought I would never in a million years see again and that was my precious blond hair. It may have been longer than I would've liked but I would take back my blonde hair more than eye color any day. Sadly, my admiration for myself didn't last long as I was shocked to find out what the fog had done to my car. It wasn't even a car but a stupid black van with the ugliest, cheapest drawing of red flames I ever laid my eyes on.

The inside of this van looked like I almost gave the Mystery Machine from Scooby Doo an Upgrade. From the Navy Blue shag carpet on the floor to the mini fridge and somewhat of a kitchen with two red bean bags in the middle and not to mention there was a bed in the back that was covered by a red curtain. Oh and I almost forgot there was even a dream catcher on the dashboard by the rearview mirror. Just Yuck!!

Anyway to make this day even worse the moment I put the key in ignition and turned it, the van wouldn't start. This has never happened to me before so in a desperate attempt to start the van, I am not proud of it rather ashamed it had come to this but I had no choice but I-I-I-I may have muttered some dirty talk to try and get it to start. Just as I finished talking dirty I heard one of my three male passengers jokingly ask

"Uhh…do you two need some privacy? Cause there's a bed and a curtain in the back." While the other men laughed and hi fived each other at the joke, I was annoyed. Looking behind me to see who out of one of my "buddies" made that joke, I noticed that this jokester looked like a Jimi Hendrix wannabe with the hair, headband, and beard pointed in the back. All he was missing was bell bottoms and a vest. Instead of all that he had the same tie dye shirt we had and had Khakis on. I responded by stating

"Hey, I know cars. Sometimes they need a little convincing, that's all." After the second and third attempt of trying to start it with no luck, it was "my" girlfr—I mean Fiancé who sat next to me, where she sweetly tugged on my jacket and asked "Can you

9

let me have a go at it?"

"Sure, knock yourself out." I answered, giving the benefit of the doubt.

She then snatched my keys from me and as I scooted over to the passenger side

I joked

"Don't be alarmed if she doesn't start right aw–" as she turned the key on the van just magically started like it was nothing. I was seething with embarrassment that she was able to accomplish what I couldn´t but I didn't say anything to her. As she backed out of the parking garage I realized that I had no idea where we were even going in the first place. So I guess this ugly Van saved me from that embarrassment too.

On the way to wherever we were going, one of the passengers asked me or rather demanded that I turn the radio on. I did what he asked as I too hate dead air. The moment I turned it on, Purple Haze by Jimi Hendrix started blaring. I was about to lower the volume but everyone started vibing to the song. *Yep. We are definitely hippies. All we need now is a talking dog.* I thought to myself while giving a big goofy smile. The loud but smooth journey to who knows where suddenly stopped when we arrived at this diner called **Bubba's Cafe.** Apparently our group are regulars here. All the staff and owner greeted us like we were family. The owner was black, bald, somewhat big boned, wearing a plain green polo shirt with black dress pants and brown shoes that was covered by an apron. He appeared to have a serious liking for me as he walked out the saloon door of the kitchen, ignoring all the other members of our group just to give me a firm handshake. I didn't understand why he was acting like this at first until I heard Renée who squealed like a little schoolgirl saying "Uncle Joey!" running over to him, pushing me aside in the process. From there I watched from the sidelines to see her act like a child as she gave him a long hug. The long hug is what made it click for me that they are in fact related which would technically make me his "Nephew in law." My "Uncle in law" asked if I was excited to come over to his brother's place and watch the big Saints game tonight.

"Sure am," I answered with a bright smile. "Wouldn't want to miss it for the world."

Renée annoyed with us and all the male bonding said

"Uncle Joe can you stop fanboyin over my man already and give us some food. We are dyin of hunger over here." Her uncle gave a big belly laugh and while wiping a fake tear "I'm not as bad as your daddy. Your daddy loves a good game of football and he would beat me before you do if I lay a hand on him." He got her there, but I guess her evil stare made him change topics. Where he asked "Okay, what will it be this time fellas?" He then passed the menus to each of us and then went one by one by name asking us what we wanted. That is a godsend for me. Before he got to me, I took a mental note of all the six other people that were in my van. The Jimmy Hendrix wannabe was this kid named Marcus; the jokester from earlier. The other two boys that were in the van with me were Randy, Dom and their girlfriends Patty and Sophie who were also in "uniform" by the tie dye shirt and orange peace symbol patch on their jean jacket.

Anyway, Renée's uncle completely skipped over me without batting an eye as to what I wanted. I was shocked and asked "Hey, what about me? You didn't ask what I wanted." He looked at me, laughed at my face and said "You always get the same thing every time you and my niece come in here. What difference does it make by me askin." Ooookayyy that was a bit rude. But whatever, I better hope I am not the one picking up the bill for all of us. Just as he left, the brass bell by the front door rang and the rest of our group joined us one by one.

This protest group of theirs was massive, I mean the group covered four booths and a couple of the barstools. I am just glad there were enough people working at the diner to help out. Seems like this diner is a family business as Reneé casually looked over at some worker cooking a burger and hollered "Hey, Caleb Yoo-hooo." This Caleb guy had a black buzz cut for hair who wore all white, looked like he wasn't older than 17 and I can tell just wanted to run and hide but couldn't as he heavily sighed, stopped for a second, looked out the little cooking window and ask "What do you want Renée? Can't you see I'm busy cookin here."

"Did you eveh ask your gal Claudia to Homecoming yet? It's coming up soon ain't it."

"Her name is Claudette and yes, I did and she said YES. Now will yuh please let me cook in peace?"

"You still with her?!" asked Marcus, flabbergasted with a big look of confusion on his face. Renée raises an eyebrow towards Marcus where he clarifies "I thought they had that big fight and broke up."

"I don't think—" she then quickly tilts her head 180 degrees and hollers " CALEB is Claudette still your gal or NAW?! "

Before Caleb could answer, Uncle Joe suddenly comes into the picture to hand our food where he looks back at him and asks "Are you talkin or yuh workin? Which one is it, boy?" I hear Caleb make an audible groan and answer "Workin" My uncle's attention turns back on us and switches topics by asking "So-o-o I take it y'all made your voices heard today?"

"Oh we voiced 'em alright. We lasted longer than last time Uncle Joe. We were out there for **TWO** hours! But we apparently overstayed our welcome and were forced to leave."

"Overstayed your welcome?" I heard Uncle Joe mutter to himself as if he didn't hear that right. So I gladly clarified by adding

"Yeah. You see, the Campus police—" before I could finish, Uncle Joe interrupted me and said almost mid shout

"That's all I need to hear boy. Don't get me **STARTED** on the Police. They have been nothin but trouble. Did you know I almost found myself in jail thanks to them back when I was 19 years old, and it was over a speedin ticket. A SPEEDING TICKET."

"We know Uncle Joe. We know." replied one black girl with the wavy hair who looked annoyed as I saw her roll her eyes just now. I recognized her as the instigator towards Renée earlier, so now I just needed a name to a face. Luckily Uncle Joe got me covered as I see him shaking his head in disappointment, turns to look at her and says almost mid shout again "The police aren't worth messin with Delilah! I suggest y'all quit while you're still ahead, before things turn **NASTY**." I am with Uncle Joe on this one as all of this is moving way too fast, not to mention risky. I mean given the time period I am in and the Vietnam War going on, anything can happen or worse someone in this group may get killed. But of course there is someone in the room who had a huge disapproval of all this and gladly voiced his opinion over the matter by shouting

"And give them the satisfaction, **HELL NAW !** "

I tilted my head to the right and saw it was Marcus who said all of this as I can tell the stress was weighing on his mind.Renée of course being the vocal leader of this group said

"Marcus, we've been over this. Violence is not the answer. We formed this group to bring peace and awareness to this ongoing war before anyone else we know gets drafted or worse killed. If you don't like what we do or say then the door's that way." pointing to the diner's front door. With steam coming off his ears, he argued "Peace, peace, peace. That's all y'all eveh talk about. I am sick of it. We can't walk on eggshells forever! I say we finally grow a pair and show em that we are not holding back and mean business. Who is with me?!" *Oh brother this is not good! His passionate speech had resonated with some of our members and some even began to cheer him on. Now Renée, the true leader of the group tried to reason with him but her words fell on deaf ears. So I guess it was my turn to save the day.*

"Marcus, as much as I want to show them cops a lesson, we can't. It's bad enough that we deal with violence in our streets, neighborhoods, not to mention a war we are in with another country. Why add more fuel to the fire? When we could do plenty of good right here without getting blood on our hands." Marcus was not interested in listening to reason. "That's all just talk!" He shouted back. "We need to take action now! If we don't, more people are going to get hurt. More people are going to die. We need to do something!" Well that didn't work. Now the situation was quickly escalating out of control until Renée diffused the situation by shouting

"Listen up, everyone! Marcus is right. We need to take action. But violence is not the way to do it. We need to show the world and this town that peaceful people are fighting for a just cause. We should organize a peaceful march at city hall that will show everyone that we will not be intimidated or silenced!" The crowd cheered in response, I turned to Marcus and asked

"What do you say about doing something like that instead?"

Without saying a word he stomps and slams the door to the diner on his way out. The moment he was gone my "fiancé" put a hand on my shoulder and said " Hopefully that will knock some sense into him." Uncle Joe chimed in to remark "That boy is just askin to get himself killed and that's a fate worse than being in the army." Once the tension in the diner finally died down, I immediately used this window of opportunity to excuse myself from the table and go to the bathroom to clear my head. Wished I could've stayed there forever but alas, this day was far from over.

It had only just begun.

Chapter 3

Keepsakes

*C*ould there possibly be another way of doing this..it's getting old. I thought to myself. As I walked into the
men's bathroom to do the wallet technique again is
so dumb…not to mention risky. Luckily it was only me in this
bathroom or else it would be very awkward very fast. I was able
to learn a lot of this Eric, including a few surprises. Firstly his
name is Eric Striker, he is 22 years old, born on July 11th 1948
and raised right here in New Orleans, Louisiana and goes to the
University of New Orleans. That and I am in September of 1970
at least that's what this car wall calendar said in the bathroom.

Huh, I guess I should give myself a pat on the back as I was right
about this being the South, the 70s and in Louisiana. Anyway,
as I stared at his driver's license more I noticed that the address
wasn't a home address but rather some Apartment Complex and
it appeared to be on Dean St. at the Rolling Meadows Apartment
complex room number 495 which is nowhere near campus.

Coming out of the bathroom, I felt like an A-list celebrity by being bombarded by people who were asking dozens of questions. In the end, I somehow managed to persuade the group that me and Renée needed some time to think about this more so we don't get ahead of ourselves. So that was the end of that and things quickly settled down and people were actually beginning to leave. Let me tell you I was so glad to be "home" after dropping off most of the people that came with us back to their campus dorms. That's good, cause I could use a break after that incident in 2002.

The fog had one more surprise waiting for me as I quickly learned that I wouldn't be alone in my apartment. It was just me and Renée left in the van after dropping off the last person Delilah off home. To my surprise, Renée begged me to go back to "our" apartment so we could quickly change to head over to her parent's house so we can "watch the big game." together.

Lucky for her, I had spent a good minute memorizing the apartment address before exiting that bathroom in the diner, so finding "our" apartment was no problem. But finding my way to her parent's house might be a different story. When I opened the door to apartment number 495. Renèe walks in like she owned the place (which she obviously did) and dumped her keys on a table and exclaimed

"Ahhh! We are home! FINALLY!"

I did the same but I looked around at my new surroundings and noticed that this apartment was small but also quite cozy.

Wouldn't mind havin a place like this once I am out of college. It had nice brown hardwood floors that were polished to a shine. The walls were painted a light yellow, and there were framed posters of various bands to even a few political figures hanging on the walls. The furniture was simple and functional consisting of a couch, sofa chair, a coffee table and a television set, There was also a small kitchenette off to one side of the main room, and appeared to be a bathroom at the end of the hall but I also noticed there was another room right next to it. Since that door was closed, I am assuming that must be the master bedroom.

THE ONLY BEDROOM IN THIS APARTMENT.

Can I sleep on the couch instead? I thought. I do not want to sleep in the same bed with this woman, if that's okay with you. I'm in a committed relationship and that is wrong. I mean what if she tries to….tries to…you know, have sex with me. But then again she does see me as her Fiancé but you never know. Anyway, I could've joined her in the bedroom to change but I decided it was best to give her some space as things could've turned out much worse for me if I wasn't careful.

So I sat on the couch despite her pleading, where I just patiently sat there and waited till she was done getting dressed. Only got up when I saw her quickly scurry to the bathroom which I know since I had sisters in my previous life that will take forever. When I got to the master bedroom (If you can even call it that) there was only one queen sized bed with orange bed sheets. I opened the big wooden closet where after I got myself dressed into this Saints jersey I found where I couldn't help but admire myself by looking at the mirror and muttering "OOOO Welcome to the gun show baby" as I began to do some muscular poses in the mirror. While I was flexing my biceps, Renée hollered from the other room.

"Are you admiring yourself in the mirror again?"

I didn't want to admit that I was, so I shouted back "NO!"

"Is what I am wearing a bit much. I know we are only seeing my parents but still."

I stopped admiring myself and hollered back saying "Let me take a look."

I heard the first steps coming closer and through the mirror, I saw her walk into the room. She looked incredible. I don't know what she was worried about. She was wearing this nice brown and rusty orange polka dot long sleeve minidress with of course the iconic Dagger collar and some black shoes so she can let everyone know we are in the Groovy Era.

"No, No it looks great on you." I said, being sincere, "Your family will love it."

"You really think so?"

"Baby. I know so."

She then to my surprise hugged me tightly, where she suddenly pulled back, started to stare at my jersey, made an audible gasp and said

"Knew I saw that jersey from somewhere, is that really—" as she stares closely at the yellow and black number 88 jersey I picked "IT IS! That's Eli's Jersey." Then menacingly stares back at me and asks "Why do you have it? Did you steal this from him?" with her eyebrows now raised.

"I didn't I–." Suddenly, I don't know what came over me but I added on by stuttering "He gave it to me before h-h–h-e-e-e you know."

"Do yuh swear on yur mother you're not lyin to me?" she asked, her eyes starting to swell. "Cause if you do I'll—"

" Renée, I swear on god, my mother and father. He gave it to me. Do you want me to take this o—"

"Nooooo!!" she shouted, interrupting me and then immediately covering her mouth, realizing she said it outloud. "Keep it on. Please." sounding very sheepish and turning into sniffles as she finished saying "He would've...wanted his fellow "Saints brotha" to wear this and wear it proudly." To my surprise, she proceeded to hug me tightly again, and I took the opportunity to squeeze and comfort her back as she clearly needed it and that's when the waterworks began to form on her round face as she started to tearfully blubber

" I miss him. I miss him so much Eric. Why is it always the good ones that have to go?" she said, blowing her nose into my shoulder.

" I don't know Renée...I do not know." While I patted her back, rocked her back and forth continuing comforting her with soothing words like saying I miss him too or something along the lines of that. When she finally calmed down she jokingly said

"Looks like I'm not ready after all. I'll be right back. Don't go anywhere." She then kissed me on my right cheek and scurried to the bathroom, slamming the door behind her.

I stood there, wondering what the heck had just happened. This had never happened to me before. Was there like some unresolved tension between Renée and Eric and who is this Eli person? Well, whoever he is, seemed to be really close with Renée. Like brother and sister close. *But that doesn't explain why I am soo–so NOT attracted to Renée. Remember Lucas.* I muttered to myself *YOU ARE in a committed relationship to one person and one person only and that is to Emily Stewart. Eric Striker is not the real you but his feelings for Renée are very strong and real. Almost as strong and real as....the girl thoughts.* Recounting my previous and horrific experience as a 1980s college girl where I can still remember the hairspray smell that Elizabeth or I had once used to this day and it was....Strawberries.

Once Renée got out of the bathroom we were all set and ready to go. But as we got to the van, she "reminded" me to go to the nearest liquor store and grab some "Dixie" for guys and get "Busch light" as that's her daddy's favorite. I then pulled out of the parking lot and drove to the nearest store to do just that.

I can't believe I am now pulling into a liquor store to get some beer without being carded is the new norm for me because Eric Striker is a 22 year old man. Sorry for being a broken record here but I am so glad I am actually near my age because going to Middle School again was horrible and it reminded me too much of my childhood. Anyway, Renée's reasoning that she kept on apologizing over and over again while I was driving was so she really and I mean really wanted me to solidify me into her family. You know, since I am the first ever "outsider" of her family. Getting out of the van, I instructed Renée to stay put, which she happily agreed and patiently waited but when I got out of the convenience store with the drinks in both hands, she decided she had enough waiting and was happily sitting in my spot…the driver's seat.

I ordered her to roll the window down and once she did, I chewed her out but oh man did it backfire as she did the same thing to me by saying "I am going to be driving on the way back due to your drinkin so what difference does it make?" Good point, but I warned her "Okay, but if—" She groaned, rolled her eyes in annoyance and interrupted me by stating " Yeah, yeah, yeah I know." she groaned in disgust "God you've been hanging out with Irving too much. I'm afraid He's rubbin off on yuh." Thinking he was another one of her or "our" friends I said

"Hey you're the one that wanted me to spend time with him. It's not my fault that he's a cool guy."

"Just get in the passenger seat you big baby before I make you walk all the way there."

You know what, I decided to have some fun with her by calling her bluff. So with an evil smirk I said "You wouldn't do it." Oh man was that a mistake because her eyebrows raised and the shocked expression with her mouth was slightly opened. She took an inhale then exhale where she calmly said

"Oh you wanna play that game huh. Okay I'll bite. Have it your way then. Your loss."

With her eyebrows furrowed down rolled the window back up. Suddenly without any warning she smiled evilly as if she had gotten an idea and before I knew it, she put the van in reverse and was backing out of the parking spot. In a panic I chased after her. Luckily for me, it didn't take long for her to change her mind as she immediately stopped the van, opened the passenger door and ordered me to get in. I reluctantly did and watched as houses and stores moved by all the while she poked fun at me much to my expense.

Chapter 4

The All-American Boy

Arriving at Renée's parent's home which was a one story house with white siding, green shutters, and a small front porch. The front yard looked to be freshly trimmed and had a basketball hoop attached on top of the garage and the house seemed to be located in a quiet suburban neighborhood. Pulling up to the driveway, I saw two teenage boys tossing a football back and forth in the front yard. One of the boys I recognized as Caleb from earlier, but I didn 't know who the other black boy was but I did know he had to be no older than 16.

The moment we got out of the car but before I could even reach for the drinks I heard someone behind me holler "Hey, Eric think fast." I turned around to see who said that and all of a sudden this small oval brown blur just darts at my face. With my quick reflexes, I was able to catch this thing just in the knick of time before it could do some serious damage. Upon closer inspection, I realized that what I had caught was a football, so I looked back at the kid who threw it and it was the 16 year old black kid standing a good distance away who I saw throwing the football around earlier. The kid with his black buzz cut hairdo wearing this yellow t-shirt that looked like he was cosplaying a bumble bee with those stripes, had blue bell bottoms that looked worse for wear and some dirty black sneakers.

I immediately figured he was related in some way, shape, or form to Renée as the resemblance between the two was quite striking. So in a playful way, I told him to go long, which he did, and threw a perfect spiral to him that only Tom Brady, the GOAT, of all football would be proud of. When he caught it, he said,

"Wow, that was some throw Eric."

"Thanks. Great....catch....dude." I said, almost out of breath. Renée being the momma bear over me shrieked

"ROGER CLANCY BOWMAN! What's the matter with YOU?! Almost breaking my Husband's nose! I want him to look good on our wedding day, not all beaten and bruised up."

While she was checking for marks or bruises on my face, Roger, who I can tell is the youngest member of the family by how he so casually brushed her remarks aside, said, "Oh relax, he caught the football didn´t he? Also he ain't your husband. Not yet. And when are you two gonna finally tie the knot?"

Renée with her mouth wide open goes "We got time. We in no rush. Ain't that right baby?" She asked, squeezing my right arm and looking at me with hearts in her eyes.

I looked down at her, smiled the best I could and answered "Yes mam." I said with an awkward laugh, "No rush at all." But for some unknown reason I blurted with a slight whisper "It's not like I already picked a best man or anything."

"You did?!" Renée shrieked. "Who is it?"

"Who is what? " I answered. Pretending I didn't hear her.

"You got cotton in your ears? I asked if you really did pick the best man already?"

"Uhhh yeahhh, I did."

I answered, squinting my eyes preparing myself for the worst but she didn't give that satisfaction, oh no. I was about to lie about who this supposed person was but she put one finger to my lips and shushed me then boldly claimed that I should "Not ruin the surprise by tellin me now, this is big news…my whole family has gotta hear this so keep your mouth shut about this until we're inside." Great just great, can this day get any worse?

Walking inside of her house with cases of her father's favorite beer on one hand and dixie on the other, I was not surprised but rather disgusted to see my old friend the green shag carpet greeting me once again. But my thoughts were quickly stopped dead in their tracks where I guess another one of Renée's siblings greeted us. The man was older, far older, like in his late 20s or possibly in his early 30s. He looked older, taller and wore a Saints football jersey number 50 where his black hair could only be loved by the Jackson five. He greeted Renée normally but before she got a word out he embarrassed her by twirling her around like a ragdoll. When he was done, put her back on solid ground and with a face glowing red from embarrassment, she meekly replied

"Hey Irving. It's good to see you too." Now when it came to me, he looked like a kid in the candy store as he cheerfully shouted

"There's my brotha from anotha motha! Wassup Eric! Give me some skin." giving me a good slap on the back that almost made me fall over.

"It's good to see yuh too Irving, how are yuh?"

"Pretty good and—" he suddenly stopped talking and noticed the beer cases I was holding and asked "Is that what I think it is?" pointing at the beer cases

"Yes sir. Got Dixie and a couple of Busch lights before we came."

"Oooo we are going to have fun **TO**-night. I'll take these off yuh hands while you two make yourself comfortable." He then took the cases of beer and headed for the kitchen. We followed him where the rest of Renée's family should be and there they were, well most of them anyway. Uncle Joe and a few other men that I didn't recognize were watching some Tv in the living room while the older women were sitting down in the dining room while one was putting the silverware and plates out on the table. "Hey Mrs. Bowman, hey everybody" I hollered as me and Renée got to the kitchen.

They all said and waved hello back except this one woman who immediately darted towards Renée. By the kisses on the cheek and the big hug greeting, I knew right away that this was her mother. Renée's Mother was a short slender woman, a couple of wrinkles on her forehead, strands of gray hair that seemed to intertwine with her black beehive hairdo and was wearing a floral pattern outfit. She didn't appear to look happy to what I greeted her as, as she gave me dagger eyes while hugging her daughter. That was a pretty good sign to me without even saying a word that I screwed up. When the hugging had stopped, she turned to me and started busting my chops by pointing out

"E-E-R-R-I-I-C-C. How many times have we gone over this so it sticks. We are Momma and Pops to you now. Your family, you gotta remember that."

"I'm sorry Momma. It's just a....It's A force of habit. That's all." I said, rubbing the back of my head in embarrassment.

"Good. Now give your momma a hug." I chuckled to myself and I did. Once the greeting hugs were established, she ordered both of us to "Come sit down at the table, food should be ready in just a few minutes." But the moment I took my first couple of steps, Renèe stopped me with one hand and coughed, signaling to me that it's now my time to shine. *Nice going Eric, you really did it to me this time. Now here is your time to shine.* I thought as I scolded myself internally. When I didn't say anything or wanted to, Renèe took the lead to say

29

"Wait just a minute Momma, before we sit down, Eric has an important announcement to make." Realizing what she was doing, I intervened and told her "Uh why don't we wait till after we have food Renée. I'm starving."

"No, especially when it has to do with our wedding. It can't wait."

Her mother puts the last silverware down on the table, stops what she is doing and gives an audible gasp as she clutches her chest and asks "You're pregnant aren't you Renée?"

Renée looking like a deer in the headlights shrieks "What! Momma I'm not expec—"

Suddenly her mom cut her off and drew her own conclusions by saying "Oh I knew it, I knew it, I knew it! That's what all women say darlin. Just wait until your father hears this." She then scurried around the dining and into the living room telling everyone who crossed her path that Renée was expecting a child while Renée who was trailing behind her, had to stop and tell those same people that she wasn't pregnant. Now I could've stayed behind and enjoyed the show but I am not lying on what I said earlier about me being hungry so against my better judgment, I followed soon after.

I caught up to them in some hallway where Momma had one hand to the sliding door that led outside while Renée with her hands on her hips said for like the **Millionth** time "Momma. I'm not pregnant. What makes you think that I am?!" Sadly her voice fell on deaf ears as her mother opened the sliding door where I saw my "Pops" for the first time out on the patio. He was tall, slim with a bald head and a black beard with a tint of gray. Who was cooking up some sweet juicy burgers on a grill. Renée's mother tapped his shoulder and said "Baby can you come inside for a minute. It's important. "

"Martha can't you see I am cooking burgers for the big game. If I leave now, the whole house is gonna burn and the Saints will lose."

"Oh I see, so you're more concerned about the Saints losing than your only daughter having a child…okay." she said with a huff. "I see how it is." Luckily this man had some sense as he took one look at his own daughter who was literally shaking in fear and brushed off Momma Bowman's craziness by stating

"Our baby girl ain't havin no child Martha. If she were, she'd be like a kid in a candy store like how you were, when we had Irving."

Finally there's someone in this household with common sense I thought to myself. After things got sorted out that she was definitely **NOT** pregnant, it was there that Renée told them that "I" had already picked a best man already without telling her and instead wanted to tell the whole family of my choosing before her mother drew her own conclusions. I guess choosing the best man is more important than juicy burgers. Her father immediately turned off the grill muttering to himself about how "they can wait." Where both of her parents followed us back to the kitchen.

31

It was there that Momma called everyone to the kitchen as I have an important wedding announcement to make.

Yeah, no pressure on me right? Where at this point in time I didn't think of a single name yet. Anyway, when all of the family gathered it was there that Renée gave them the spiel on how I made my mind on the perfect best man without consulting her and said it was best to tell the whole family. Thinking of a way to get out of this situation without things getting ugly I decided to wing it and made the bold decision to name this Elijah fellow as the best man. As he seemed to have the most impact on Renée and it is someone who she clearly loved more than anything even Eric. If anyone asks I'll just make up a sob story to really sell it so whenever Elijah gets back from the army he'll know and be either happy or mad with Eric. Not me. So I took a deep breath and announced to them that

"Renée is right, I had made the decision for who the best man would be at our wedding for way too long now. I-I never had a chance to tell him in person but my best man is Eli—"

Before I finished saying his name, everyone in the room gasped, suddenly Renée's mother who was in tears let out this big whale of a sob and blubbered

"Elijah! " Where her mother got up and ran to her room, ugly crying the entire way there for everyone to hear and we all heard her door slamming. The whole family started to murmur amongst themselves in pure disbelief and that's when Renèe looking frantic asked me

"Were you seriously going to choose my big brother over your best friends."

Are you telling me that they were related all this time and I had no idea?!

That's a pretty big deal and—wait…she used the word, WERE. Like in the past tense. You mean to tell me that he DIED!?! That's even worse! I thought he was a best friend that was still in the army. I should've known especially when Renée said "Why is it always the good ones that have to go." Makes so much sense, now that I think of it. Nervously, I answered while rubbing the back of my head "Uhh, uhm, yeah I was. I was…I was uh kinda hoping he would be the one to tell you actually." as I nervously laughed. "There was never a good ti—" suddenly Renée hugged me tight.

Woah, I wasn't expecting that. I guess you can say I left a lasting impression on this family. It took a while to compose ourselves but I think we are all ready to sit down at the table and finally eat. While waiting for "Pops" to bring in the burgers, I noticed an empty chair to the left of me. I knew right then and there, that spot was meant for Elijah. Everything felt so…so different now. Like the fun and joking all died, the moment I had brought him up. Even when we were eating, only a couple phrases were spoken like "pass the salt." and etc. To this day I still feel guilty bringing him up like that, knowing now that they were clearly still grieving.

To avoid any further discomfort for the family, I decided that it would be best to shift the conversation to sports, knowing full well that Elijah was a big fan of the Saints. So I asked if anyone would care to wager on the game tonight. This seemed to spark interest with the younger members of the family and really eased a lot of the tension. The whole family is even starting to talk and laugh like normal again as most of them even wanted to join in on the wager. Hell, even Renèe threw down a few singles at the table to get a betting jar going.

Seems like my idea really took off. I think this deserves a pat on the back. Everybody here wanted to write on a piece of paper what they thought the score would be at the end of the game. There were so many papers in the mason jar that we ended up having to include four mini winners (One for each quarter in the game) where the winners would get like two dollars for winning while the main winner would get the rest of the cash prize. If you're wondering, no I didn't cheat as I'm not the smartest man in the world or a Saints fan, okay and guessed like everybody else. Besides the closest I've seen to old football, is highlights from Joe Montana and Walter Payton. So with that I began to watch and enjoy the game with "the boys". This actually reminded me of a lot of my friends. Especially how we were all shouting at the tv. But I'll never forget when during the second quarter, Renèe's father shouts

"Man, what is he doin!" as I then watched him put his bottle of beer with such force on the glass table that the beer started to jump out. "Throwin the ball like that. Is he asking for them to get an interception?"

His anger lasted for only a moment as I guess he took notice of only my second empty beer bottle and hollered for Renèe who was in the kitchen

"Renée, will you be a dear and get your man a beer from the fridge?" I put my hand out to stop him and replied

"Pops, I can grab myself one. Renée doesn't have to do that for me."

"Nonsense Eric. This is a man's game. You stay here, and let the woman do all the work."

I was about to say something but Renèe stopped and reassured me

"It's okay Eric. I don't mind grabbing you one. You deserve it." as I looked back and saw her grabbing another bottle of Dixie from the fridge and slammed the door shut. She then walked with a pep in her step over to me and handed the green bottle but not before giving me a kiss on the cheek first. Oh I can get used to this. But there's still something on my mind that doesn't sit right. My "Pops" seemed to know what was wrong with me right away and asked what was wrong but before I could get a word out he surprised me by saying

"I know, son. You don't have to say it. I miss him too. We all do. Ain't that right fellas." Looking at all the guys. They then expressed how much they miss Elijah and his father added "Besides, you and Eli were always the biggest Saints fans out of all of us."

This then turned into a bonding moment for all the guys where every male member of Renèe's family told at least one funny story they had of Elijah Bowman. Out of all the stories that I heard of the man, my favorite story had to be from Renèe's youngest brother; Roger, where he recalled a time back when Eli was in high school in like Junior or Senior Year and was the only single man out of his friend group. One of them had bet $10 that he couldn't get a girl to walk home with him while they watched. You know what Eli did. He brought a girl home from school but it was not just any girl. It was Renèe because his friend didn't say it had to be a stranger. She only agreed on doing this in the first place because Eli promised to split the money with her if she agreed to be dolled up as if she went to Sunday School for a day.

You know, as a way to seemingly make her unrecognizable as I got the impression she was more of a tomboy back in highschool.I can only imagine his friends' face when it was revealed that Renée was walking home from school with him. I laughed with all the guys hearing that heartfelt story. Hearing these family's amazing stories about the man, myth, and legend made me wish I could meet Eli myself. He sounded like a cool guy. He's like one of those people that you could honestly chill and have a beer with. If there was a medal or competition for who's the most All-American, he would have my vote 110%.

I learned of his big heart and how he sometimes went out of his way to help those in need....kinda like me. From what I am hearing he was on track to be the first ever doctor of this family... that was until The Draft Lottery came and ruined everything. The Bowman family were VERY vocal about their distaste for it and detailed the gut retching blow as they saw it on TV and seeing Eli's face when he received his rejection letter from a school they could just barely afford the day of the draft. But now that he's gone, it seems like Renée, Roger, and Irving all have big shoes to fill. I don't know what position or rank Eli was in the army but I can only assume that with his medical experience, he must've been a Combat Medic. That's probably the worst and most dangerous job you can get in the army.

As I stood there, frozen and feeling the weight of so many eyes on me, I was then assaulted by a cacophony of voices, all asking me the same question: "Do you remember" It was as if I were standing in a cave or at the bottom of the Grand Canyon, and the sound was echoing off the walls. I couldn't make out any individual voices, the collective effect was overwhelming where I just blurted " I-I-I can't." Everyone gasped. "It's hard to name just one. Let alone a—" suddenly my "Pops" gets up from his brown recliner and pats me on the back saying "You don't have to tell us if you don't want to. We understand."

That didn't make me feel better whatsoever but anything is better than being called a liar or something worse. So I'll gladly take the sympathy card. I nodded and the family was all back to normal once the football game was back on. The rest of the game was awesome even though the Saints lost. Everyone was surprised on who won the big cash prize though. It was Renèe. Who didn't even watch the game. Once the main winner and runners up were revealed, which were me, Roger, Renée's cousin Caleb and Uncle Joe, the party seemed to die down but there is still one thing I want to do before I want to leave this place and that is to go pay a visit to Elijah's room.

I have to.

Chapter 5

Wake Up Call

So many questions are lingingering in my head as to why Renée's family hid all photos of their precious Elijah from me. Did they remove them before I walked through the front door or the moment they learned of his passing. Looking around the house I tried searching for a photo of any kind of him just in case they had missed one but I had found none. I guess a photo of him must trigger painful memories just by even looking at him. I'm sorry but I want to see him for myself even if I have to tear down the whole house looking for one. Instead of imagining what he looked like. It's exhausting.

I knew I had to be sneaky while doing it as I didn't want anybody to notice what I was up to. So I snuck past Renée's family and went to the hallway where I know the bedrooms and bathrooms must be and two failed attempts of opening the wrong room, I felt like I was getting close.

Heading to another door at the end of the hall, I finally found the bedroom I was looking for or in this case...two bedrooms. There was a dresser against the wall between the two beds and on top of the dresser was a clock and a lamp with each two separate closets. On the left side of the room was a boys bed with its navy blue striped bed sheets with what appeared to be a varsity jacket hanging on a hanger outside his wooden closet, a desk that had a framed photo and on the right side where you walk in was a-a-a GIRL'S BED with a plain yellow pastel color for bed sheets and a brownish golden teddy bear sitting on top of the bed.

No wonder Renée got so emotional when I mentioned her brother's name as she literally slept and lived in the same room as the man for most if not all of her life. Only thing to do now is to close the door and explore. Once I did that, I discovered that he was a highschool graduate of '63 at least that's what I could make out on the dark blue varsity jacket that was hanging just outside his closet. But on his desk was a colorized photo of a man in his dark green army uniform. Oddly enough, he looked like Renée if she were a man with the military hair, hat, and dark green uniform. As I was admiring the photo, the bedroom lights suddenly came on and I heard a voice from behind me say "Knew it would only be a matter of time till you showed your face here."

In a panic, I quickly put the photo of him on the desk, turned around and saw it was only Renée with her face looking pale, leaning on the door frame. She then closed the door behind her and reassured me

40

"Don't worry, it's just me. My parents or anyone else doesn't know you're in his room....or... our room yet. So take it easy." Phew, that's a relief. I cautiously asked her

"How'd you know I would be here?"

"Well, I couldn't help but overhear what you had said about Elijah, I can't believe my family thought it would be a good idea to start interrogating you." where she glared evilly behind her and started shaking her head before continuing saying "I don't know what they were thinkin. But I guess Eli was right. Once an outsider. Always an outsider." I am starting to see why Renée and everyone looks up to him so much as he always had something to say even if you didn't want to hear it. I was about to say something but Renée beat me to it and added, "Once I heard you say you can't remember, I knew you had to clear your head and talk to him and what better place than here."

She walked over to his desk and picked up the photo of Elijah in his army uniform. "Did you know this is the last photo that we have of him. This photo. Right here." showing me the picture of him right in my face then gently placing it back on the desk, she looked at me and with a straight face continued "After he was shipped off to basic training, he sent letters back home saying that he wished my momma was there cookin so the men could have good food instead of the slob they were served." She grabbed a box of tissues to blow her nose and continued saying "Once bootcamp was over, is when I could tell he changed. In the beginning he told us funny conversations he had heard, told

41

personal life stories of his army buddies and those that he had saved. But as the days went by, he stopped telling us those stories and began telling us new ones that were scary. He first started to tell us how horrible this place is from the smell, weather, and violence. Then he told us how he blamed himself for failing to save the life of his best friend who got shot as they had gotten ambushed somewhere in the jungle where he ended up tripping over a goddamn root trying to get to him. Only to be held back by one of his own men claiming that "man was dead before his head hit the ground." and how they didn't want to lose their only medic. It was a miracle, Elijah survived that day."

She paused to take a deep breath and added "The ones he couldn't save hit him the hardest. Sometimes he swears he hears them calling out to him in his dreams. The last letter he shared with us was another complaint of the same old nickname they gave him. Most of the boys would call him "Doc" but he hated that one with a passion, he preferred being called "Giggles" as he always did say that "Laughter is the best medicine." even in the darkest of times, he always wanted to make people laugh." She awkwardly chuckled to herself before continuing "Before he and the boys had to go on yet another dangerous mission, he promised us that he would try to write tomorrow when he has time and that he loves and misses all of us." She then paused to take a deep breath and continued "But Eric I'll never forget the day the letters had stopped coming in. Remember I was helping out Momma in the kitchen while you and all the boys were out in the backyard playing football when I heard that knock at the door.

I knew right then and there he was gone and was never coming back." Renèe's voice cracked as she said all of this, and I could tell that she was trying to hold back tears. I reached out and put my arm around her, and she leaned into me. We stood there in silence for a moment, both lost in our thoughts.

Finally, Renée cleared her throat and said, "I'm so glad you're here. We all are, even if most of us don't tell you to your face. I know this hasn't been easy for you as you two shared a deep bond." she paused, sighed and then trying to hold back her tears again blurted "It's hard to believe he's really gone. Why it feels like yesterday he was here eating dinner with us an–an–and" Renée couldn't hold back her tears anymore and let out this whale just like her mother did earlier. All of the sadness in the air made me shed a few tears and sniffled myself as I gave her a hug and said softly.

"You know he's not really gone." She looked at me confused when I said "He will always live on in here." tapping my heart.

Renée smiled sadly. "I know. I feel it too."

We embraced for another hug, after we were done Renée stated

"We should get out of here. My parents are probably worried sick by now. Remember last time."

"Yeah, Yeah, I remember."

43

I followed Renée out the door and took one last look of their childhood room before shutting the door. The moment I shut it, we both saw Rodge walking towards us in a hurry and said "There you two are, we were starting to get worried especially when we heard crying."

"Everything is fine. Roger. We just had a lot to talk about." she replied with her head gesturing to the door we just came out of.

" I know what you mean." Roger said looking at the door then quickly back at us and revealed that "I had stuff that I wanted to get off my chest too before you guys stopped by." With his eyes now glaring at the floor. It was at that moment that Renée hugged Rodge dearly and tearfully said "Oh Rodge, you can always vent and talk to me or Eric about anything, we are here for you. Ain't that right, Eric."

"That's right," I replied jumping into the conversation "we are all here for you Roger. If you have anything bothering you, whether it's school or something else, you can always hang out with us. Just let one of us know and we'll gladly make time out of our day for you." I replied as I was now beginning to understand what Elijah's legacy was to the family. Roger started to sniffle and hugged me and whispered in my ear

"You sounded just like Elijah right there."

"Well, what can I say we were pretty tight." I whispered back to him. This made Roger give a big goofy smile along with a chuckle and said "I'll think about it. Thanks Eric, I really needed that."

I don't know if it was something I said or maybe it was my kind gesture towards Renée's little brother Roger but whatever I did made her act all lovey dovey with me by linking arms as we headed back to the living room to meet her parents. She never left me out of her sight either. But she was still adamant on being the one driving home when it was only me and her left in the house beside her parents and little brother so I don't know what was up with her.

On the drive back to her or I guess "OUR" place, I was so scared of what she might want to do since it's just the two of us in an apartment. ALONE. I tried to distract myself for as long as I could by watching tv but the moment I turned the tv on, Renée said that we have a big day tomorrow with the group and we can't miss it. I groaned and turned the TV off and cautiously joined her in the master bedroom. I immediately went to go change with Renée soon following. I don't know if it's Eric's sick mind but I was tempted to look at her while she was changing even if it was for a moment.

That's when I shook my head and reminded myself that I am in a relationship with Emily Stewart who've I have known for almost three years and I would have you know it's considered adultery in some places and religions including mine. THAT'S RIGHT FOLKS. Ever since I knew Emily, I realized throughout my journey thus far that she is the only girl that I want to spend the rest of my life with. No matter how many other women I've come to know. But how am I going to—oh I know. I will use the argument that me and Renèe had earlier today as a perfect excuse. So the moment she sat down in her—her lovely green baby doll frilly nightgown and as she layed in bed turning the night lamp off, is the moment I got up. But to my horror she turned the light back on, latched onto my neck like an octopus and pulled me back to bed. Where she then sweetly asked

"E-E-E-r-r-r-i-i-i-c-c-c where are you goin at this hour?"

"The couch." I answered while slowly putting her arm off my neck. But the moment I thought I was free, I got up but she latched on again but this time only onto my arm and sat me back down saying

"The couch? Hun. Nothing is on at night, you know that." as she started to yawn. "So crawl back to bed with me."

"I know that. I know. I'm just gonna sleep there since we did have that big fight remember."

"That's what you're so tense about. Baby there's no need for that, I'm not mad at you."

"You're not." I said petrified and frozen with fear that my plan is not working.

"Noooo." as she scooted closer and forced me to sit back down on the bed. She continued " In fact, I couldn't be any happier, knowing my future husband made the difficult choice in choosing my brotha Eli as the best man for his wedding than anybody else. He would've been to the moon hearing this."

"What would have happened if I didn't choose him?" I curiously asked.

"Well, my family and I would've been deeply hurt but at the end of the day would have respected your decision and reasoning on the person you had in mind." she answered. "But enough talkin, let's relax and enjoy this quiet evenin we have together." as she slowly turned my face towards hers and as I felt hands wrapped around my neck, Renée smiled....and locked lips with me. *Oh brother. What have I done?*

After a few smooches, I pulled her away and nervously laughed saying "I guess I made the right choice." Where she happily continued to lock lips with me to get her point across. I had enough and broke away from her kissing. She pouted when I stopped but I explained how that's enough for one night, told her sweet dreams and turned the lamp light off. Renée must've been super bummed as her lamp light was still on for a good thirty seconds but she turned it off too and we both finally went to sleep. The next morning I almost had a panic attack as I woke up to the sound of someone's rhythmic breathing. I slowly turned my head to the right to see what the sound was and to my horror, I saw Renée still fast asleep, latched onto my waist.

With her head snuggled right under my armpit. I was so scared that I didn't have the heart to move her. I just laid back in bed, staring at the ceiling, wondering how I am going to wiggle out of her grasp without waking her up. *Maybe I should push her away,* I thought. *No.* I thought, scolding myself. *I am scared of what she might do to me when she wakes up. Maybe I should try calling for help. Help?! Okay that is probably the stupidest idea I have ever had.*

Who in their right mind is going to save me when I am technically married to this woman. Not to mention I am in an apartment for crying out loud so who knows what strange people are living here.

Yet she looked so adorable sleeping that I just couldn't have the heart to move her. So in the end, I just layed back in the bed staring at the ceiling and when I got bored of that I turned to face Renèe and prayed that she woke up so I could get out of here. Luckily she did, the moment I turned to face her, she had this goofy smile and softly spoke

"Morning sleepyhead, how'd you sleep?"

"Like a baby. You?"

"Same. But I just couldn't stop thinking about last night. Even now… " as Renée's voice trailed off as she blushed and looked away but only for a moment.

"What was so special about last night?" I asked. "All we did was kiss."

"I know babe, but whatever trick you pulled up your sleeve last night, keep it up. I mean you were always a good kisser…but this—this felt different. Like if you weren't so careful I would've let you take it one step further if you hadn't stopped" Renée blushed and laughed awkwardly. Outwardly I was calm, collected and—ahhh man you caught me. I went to the moon! Looking back now, I guess I was so happy to hear her say that I was a good kisser that it actually made me blank on what she said after which really came to bite me in the butt later. Anyway, I immediately acted surprised, and asked "I did?!" Where she then nodded.

Renée is the first girl other than Emily to say that I am a good kisser. Cathy Miller back when I was Gary Walter doesn't count as her first ever boyfriend was Gary. So I guess it is TRUE after all. Buuuutttt I couldn't let Renée know all this, for obvious reasons so I decided to mask my reason as to why by saying

"Well, I did say I had a lot of practice." as I now started to stretch my arms and back.

"Hmmm kissing another woman sure does sound like a lot of practice to me." Renée sarcastically remarked.

Well technically, it's three other women if you count Emily... but who's counting? Seems like I have more in common with Eric than I thought. Now as we were sitting down and eating breakfast together, the phone rang. "I'll get it." Renée answered, walking over to the wall phone in the kitchen. "It's probably my mom on the other end, checking to see if we made it home last night." When I watched her pick up the phone I overheard a girl on the other line that didn't sound anything close to her mother say

"Hey Renée, It's me Delilah there's been a slight change of plans, can you and Eric meet me outside the library on campus? There's something important that you two gotta see." and hung up.

Chapter 6

Misfits

"What was that about?" I asked finishing up this waffle that Renée had made for me. She turned to me and answered

"Beats me, but that was Delilah on the other end and she asked us to meet her outside the library on campus. She sounded urgent."

"Well what are we waiting for, let's go." as I slammed my napkin on my empty plate.

We then got ready and I drove us to campus but Renée wanted to park at Delilah´s dorm first as she had to grab some things that she left last time she was there. Whatever, but with her helpful guidance to where that was as I "claimed" I haven't been there in a while. Which I guess must´ve been true as she actually gave me directions to her place where I then had to wait in the van for her to grab something from her dorm room. Now when she got out,

I joined her and locked my van as we proceeded to make the long walk to the campus library.

Being alone with her felt different. This is not my first time hanging out with a girl before but she reminds me a lot of Emily. It's starting to scare me. Like for example Renée told or rather begged me to take the long scenic route on our way to campus. She then became very "nostalgic" by grabbing me by the arm and leading me to the spot where " I had " popped the question. She then even begged me to go down on one knee to ask her again. I reluctantly got down on one knee and popped the question, she laughed and said "YES!" and gave me the longest smooch on the lips of my life that was followed by a hug soon after.

She then grabbed me by the arm and I was guided to this old willow tree where she told me about the time where she and "Eric" saw one kid get so high on acid, he thought he could "fly like Superman" and fell down from a tree branch where they had to be the ones to call an ambulance for the poor fool. Meanwhile Emily Stewart has the memory of an elephant too, like she remembers the first song we ever listened to together when we weren't even a couple. I even forgot about it until she reminded me when I took her somewhere special on our 2nd anniversary date, that she casually brought it up.

I was surprised that she remembered the exact moment she fell in love with me as it was the day I helped her move into her new home. I thought it was when we first locked eyes but I was wrong. It was the moment when we were in her room and how I took time out of my day when I got done with helping her father unload all the boxes, where instead of leaving, she was surprised on how I actually took time to help unpack some things in her room like getting her record player out of a box, hooked it up in her room and jammed out to a Led Zeppelin song called Good Times Bad Times which the cover album was that of a blimp to make sure that it worked is when she fell hard for me.

That and her goofy personality alone and hobbies are what made me so drawn to her in the first place. She's a gamer nerd like me but also loves singing and playing guitar too. Having interesting hobbies can be said the same about Renèe who I remember being told to stop dead in my tracks as she had a spotted an Ivory-colored woodpecker right behind me and whined like a little kid on how she left her camera at our apartment as she needed to take a photo of that bird for her lovely little scrapbook.

I asked what birds she still has left and with a big goofy grin gave me a short list of the type of birds that live here and ones that she had not taken a photo of yet. Also her laugh and smile are quite contagious as I watched her walk ahead of me and spin around like she was one of those princesses with the big ballgown but instead of that, she was in her green floral dress and matching headband belting out loud on how much she loves nature an— oh my goodness, I'm falling for her…aren't I? This is not good.

Being smitten with her is one thing but I gotta remind myself that I'm not the one in love with her…Eric is and that's the thing that is being taken out of context as she doesn't see me as me, the real me. Now does she? Thought so. Anywho once we arrived on Campus grounds again, I followed Renée to the library and as we got closer I saw the same girl with the wavy black hair in a black striped shirt with blue jean shorts and had white go-go boots where she immediately ran to Renée, hugged her tight, while I just got a simple head nod of acknowledgement. Anyway, she broke free from the hug, looked annoyed as she asked us

"What took you two so long?" as I saw her arms crossed and impatiently tapping her foot. Renée bit her lip and answered

"Sorry Delilah, we took the scenic route."

"Ohhhh....my bad. I didn't know." she replied, sounding sheepish.

I didn't want to be reminded of that so I jumped into the conversation and asked

"So what's the big emergency?"

"It's this." as she guided Renée and I inside the library where we took a left turn and at the end of the hallway was a board with thumbtacks holding a dozen or so flyers where one in particular caught my eye, it was a red flier with a black silhouette of a flying monkey holding a sign that says to "Stop the War" on the top left side and on the middle of the right side of the paper was another flying monkey hanging upside down holding a sign on the right side that says "Make a Difference." In the middle of all that, there was this black writing and it read something like:

HEY YOU! Do YOU want to Make the World a better place and Actually GET RESULTS. WE ARE THE FLYING MONKEYS and through the power of cooperation and communication, we can accomplish anything we put our mind to.

The Flying Monkeys Are Here and Here To Stay and We need your help to make our vision and club a success.

IF YOU WANT to hear more of what you can do to help.

Come join us tomorrow at 2pm at Doug´s Bakery where you can get free Coffee and Donuts. We Hope to See You There!!

That was some flier, I thought to myself. I can see why this had caught Delilah´s attention too as she took it off the thumbtacked wall board and gave it to us saying

"I saw "**Someone**" putting these bad boys all over campus and they awfully reminded me of our own club and guess who that someone was?"

"Who?" me and Renée asked in unison.

"Marcus." she replied with her face set in stone.

Marcus?! I'm sorry but that Jimmi Hendrix wannabe seems to be the last person in this group to do something this drastic. Sure, he was upset about us not taking enough "action" but I just figured he was just "in touch with his feelings" as that seemed to be the common trend in the 60s into the 1970s. By the looks of our shocked faces Delilah continued saying that

"I warned him about what he was doing and the wedge of our friendship he was creating but he just wouldn't listen."

55

Renée looked like she wanted to hurt somebody and she with an evil look demanded to ask Delilah "Where is he?!"

"Over by the Cafeteria, I think he's putting more of his fliers up."

Renée grabbed my hand without any warning, squeezed it pretty hard and we headed in that direction while I looked at Delilah who only mouthed "Sorry" before we took off. We spotted Marcus putting a new flier like Delilah had said he would be and Renée looked like she was ready to burst like someone popping a zit. I swear her shouting could be heard from across the room when she belt out

"What the hell are these fliers?! Marcus, we didn't ask you to hand these out." as we speed walked towards him.

"I know." He calmly answered, diffusing the tense situation. " These flyers are mine. Do yuh like it? I wrote them myself." feeling quite proud of himself.

"Your flier?" I asked, Puzzled. "Yeah, don't you mean our flier?" Renée chimined in. "Noooo it's my NEW club that I started. Eveh since you two gave me my last warning so to speak, I decided to go start my own group called "The Flying Monkey Committee "

"Like those creatures in The Wizard of Oz?" I asked

"Yeah." He chuckled. "Like the movie..you like the name Eric?"

I was gonna say something but my "fiancé" finger pointed at me and fiercely ordered me that "He's not gonna answer that, if he knows what's good for him." As she started to evilly stare at me assuming I was. Which I'm not…but still. Instead I asked

"What's the meaning behind the name of "The Flying Monkey Committee" anyway."

"Change…for the better, no matter what. That's what it means Eric."

"That's dumb and doesn't even make sense." Renèe chimed in to complain. I agreed with her on that one. But according to Marcus

"It don't have to be, when I know plenty of people round here who like me aren't too stoked at the government for what they did and join my club. Instead of doing whatever it is you two were planning." He then looked around to see if people were watchin us and when they weren't he said "Between you and me "The Revolutionary White Doves '' sounds more like a name for a "high school mascot." than a group of protesters." *That's the name of our club?!* I am sorry but I couldn't help it and let out a few childish giggles before I got elbowed in the gut by my loving partner Renèe. According to her, laughing wasn't the right move. Renèe with her face glowing red in embarrassment defended her reasoning by stating

"The name is a symbol for peace and compassion."

"That's so bull. I can smell it from a mile away." Marcus replied. He then changed the subject by trying to bribe us into joining his little club by suggesting " We are always welcoming new members you know. Just for the hell of it, I 'll even make you two our new Treasurer and Secretary." He then reaches his hand out and asks "What do yuh say?"

Renée blankly stares at his hand and his face then slaps his hand away and right when she looked like she was getting ready to slap him silly, I grabbed that hand and chimed in to say

"No thanks, we're good. We are not interested in joining your little fan club." I let go of Renée's hand where she looked at me, grinned and nodded in approval.

"You two are going to regret that. Why I bet before the end of the new week is OVER….everyone on CAMPUS will know and FEAR the Flying Monkey Committee. Where Peace and Justice will finally be restored." he then breathed in and out through his nostrils before shouting "JUST...YOU...WAIT!" as he finger pointed and threatened us…before stomping away.

I thought that would be the last we would see and hear of Marcus and the "Flying monkey Committee" but I was wrong.

VERY

Wrong.

Nothing would prepare me for what happened next.

Chapter 7

War

Ever since those heated words were exchanged between us, nothing good has become of it. The following Monday night, during our group meeting in some college classroom we noticed that out of the Thirty people we had in the group, only Twenty Two of them had shown up. It was small but definitely noticeable. It got so much worse after that. The very next day we put out flyers for our fundraiser to save the trees that was going to be held at the Bubba´s Cafe that upcoming weekend rather than protesting at city hall or on campus as we all unanimously agreed that saving our image is important. But to our surprise, we discovered that after two hours of putting them up, every single one of our flyers were either vandalized or had gone missing.

When I say "Vandalized" I mean our flyers were covered up with "The Flying Monkey Committee" flyers instead; some of which were even crossed out in black sharpie! We even found a couple of ours crumbled up and stuffed in nearby trash cans. This left us no choice but to retaliate by doing the exact same petty thing to them and that my friends is how the **WAR** between the "Revolutionary White Doves" and the "Flying Monkey Committee" began.

Soon the pettiness we had towards each other turned into threats. The catch is that only one of us was making them. It wasn't us as we advised our group to not listen to them but some of the flying monkeys members made it their mission to intimidate us by meeting us outside our classes or even out and about on the street! Me and Renée tried telling our club members to stand their ground, ignore them and most importantly don't let your frustration out on them as you need to be the better person. This advice seemed to have worked but in the back of my head, I knew it was only a matter of time till one of our club members cracked and when that happens then oh lord please help us.

I always thought it was my fault when that tragic day came that I didn't do anything to prevent it. Looking back, I see that it wasn't my fault as the fight between The Revolutionary White Doves and The Flying Monkey Committee was always inevitable. Now I truly believe that Marcus was not totally happy with our group and was interested in being more aggressively active and was looking for a good time to move on.

Anyway, back to my story, so it is now a lovely Thursday, **September 24th 1970.**

On that day, Renée and I weren't with Delilah, Owen, and Dom when it happened in some alleyway. We were actually nearby enjoying some grub at Bubba's café on a "lunch date" I came up with as a sweet way to cheer Renée up and get her mind off of the hassle of running a club and her problems with Marcus. There we were just casually drinking and enjoying our time together as a "couple" when suddenly the diner door was roughly swung open and I saw a shadowy figure dressed in black run towards us. As the figure got closer I realized that it was none other than Delilah who came in and said trying to catch her breath "There's....there's....a-a-a-a"

"A what? A **Fight** Happening?!" I asked

"Yes!" Delilah shrieked. "Just a block away in the alleyway on the left. Please help them Eric."

I told her that I would and ordered Renée to stay there and calm Delilah down while I went to investigate. I ran to the alleyway as fast as I could. I brushed off and shoulder checking several people in the process but I didn't care. As I got closer, I saw a white van coming from an adjacent alleyway hitting a trash can and taking off like a speeding bullet. Getting to where the van took off from, I heard someone call out "Eric!" followed by a loud cough and groan. I turned in that direction. There I spotted one of our club members Owen with his messy brown hair, freckles and looked like he just got into a fight and lost horribly. As his school shirt was torn and bloody, had bell bottoms and was leaning against a wall coughing with one hand on his head. It was there that I asked him "What happened? Who did this to you?"

"Me, Dom and Delilah were just out explorin the city when these guys in ski masks came from out of nowhere and grabbed her. We saw one of 'em cover her mouth while she was screaming for help as they led her to some alleyway." He then gave this loud horse cough and continued "We found them and managed to get Delilah free but they got us pretty good. Them cowards. I'm gonna kill Marcus for this."

"Are you 100% positive it's Marcus and his gang?" He gave me a look and said

"That Jimi Hendrix fucker took his ski mask off and told us to give you and Renée a warning before leaving us here."

"What'd he say?" I asked. Owen looked down at the ground ignoring me. "Owen, look at me" as I turned his head "What did he say?!"

"He says…" as he gives another loud cough " to stay out of his way before you find yourself … looking like…him." and gave another loud cough before slowly pointing at this lifeless body lying on the pavement just a few feet away from me. I immediately turned around to see what he was pointing at and I immediately recognized that lifeless body. It was Dom's. One of Eric's good friends. "Dom!" I shrieked as I ran towards him where I knelt down and put my ear on his chest. Thankfully he was alive. Seems like he had just been knocked out cold. Thank God.

I don't want to have another dead body ingrained in my head. One is plenty. But there's something you should know. I didn't tell you this sooner but for these past two treacherous weeks, Dom has really proven himself to be quite a reliable and a fun guy to be around especially at bars. Yes you heard that right, I am using my new found reflection's age to my advantage as who knows when I will be a 22 year old man again. Anyway, it may have been the stress of this rivalry or just seeing an unconscious body but for whatever reason I just broke down and cried at Dom's chest and had to be pulled away by Renée once the ambulance and police officers arrived. As Dom and Owen were being put on a stretcher I muttered to myself that Marcus and his group would pay for this while the police officers were taking witness statements.

I wondered when this stupid war between us would finally be over and when I would get out of here. That was not a reality because later that day, Renée and I were asked to come to the University's Security Superintendent's office and were told that since I didn't get a clear look at the perpetrators or the getaway vehicle's license plate it's really just hearsay against Owen's word against Marcus' group. It didn't help when they were being interviewed that the true instigators of the fight were theater majors...so one could say they put up quite an oscar worthy performance....and won. Now as for our members, they weren't expelled...exactly. We were left with no choice but to kick them out of our club or else as Renée and I being the group leaders would get punished and we didn't want that.

Have any of these people heard innocent until proven guilty? Is that even still a thing? We thought the rest of our group would understand but we were wrong. A lot of members in our group were angered by our decision and blamed us for not sticking up for them but for ourselves. Most if not all of the angered members decided to leave our club for good not wanting to join either club while others went to join *The Flying Monkey Committee.* Despite what Dom, Delilah and Owen had to say too.

Now here me and Renée were just idly standing by this board where the service learning hours were posted, discussing what the plan for retaliation would be. Without physically harming them.

If things couldn't get much worse than you're wrong. The following day after class, me and Renée were standing by this board of flyers in the hallway and were discussing what our next plan of action should be to reel most of our club members back when suddenly one of the campus officers by the name of Sgt. Carter or at least that's what it said on his police name tag walked over and asked us what we were planning. Renée casually told him that "We weren't planning anything and were just talking."

Of course given our new found reputation and sabotages throughout campus these past two weeks, he wasn't going to let that slide. He asked again, this time sounding more sharp and threatening. I wasn't going to let this happen so I jumped in and started to say "We were just talkin about...." before drifting off as I noticed the flier of a soup kitchen looking for volunteers. This seemed to be a perfect excuse for getting him off our backs and finished by saying "Just talking about volunteering at the local soup kitchen on that flier over there." pointing at the orange paper with a picture of a kitchen in the background with a cartoonish hand shake.

Renée looked at me confused but quickly caught on to what I was doing and told Officer Carter that was exactly what we were doing and to move along. But he wouldn't back down without a fight and rudely suggested "If you two were volunteering why haven't you signed the flier to make it official? Isn't your group all about taking action?" with a raised eyebrow. I hate to say this, I really do but Officer Carter made a good point. I tried to come up with a lame excuse to get out of it, like how we don't have a pen on us but the officer being ever so "generous", handed Renée one from his left shirt pocket and said "Ladies, go first." Renée did not like to hear that as I swear I saw steam coming out of those ears.

"There!" an annoyed Renée exclaimed as she finished signing her name in dramatic fashion. "You happy?!"

"Very." he replied in an evil like chuckle. "Now it's your turn." looking directly at me. I rolled my eyes at him and snatched Renée's pen from her and signed "my" name right under hers. Once we were done with the signing, officer Carter thanked us for doing our "community service" but before leaving he told me to "Keep the pen, it may come in handy later." and took off. Renée and I then went on to another one of our classes.

I didn't know what he meant at the time until it was during the middle of a lesson in one of my classes when two campus police officers abruptly came in unannounced, called me out by name where I was ordered to head into the President of the University's office. Once there I see Renée in a chair facing the main desk and the president sitting down with Officer Carter and another officer standing behind him like bodyguards. I was then ordered to take a seat next to Renée where the man in a blue suit explained to us that

" It's nothing personal, kids, but Officer Carter told me that you two were making plans to volunteer at the local soup kitchen and I have approved him to be present for the entirety of your volunteering hours or as he put it." He then paused to quote 'So there ain't no funny business happenin.' Am I hearin you right Carter?" We both looked at the man who nodded and answered "Yes sir, that's right." The president then turned to us and asked us "Now how many hours do you two plan on being there?" I for one didn't want or plan on staying there any longer than I needed to but to be safe and to convince the lovely officer I said "Two." Now at the same time my partner was thinking the exact same thing but opposite to what I wanted because she said "Three." Right...after...me. I looked at her like she was crazy and exclaimed

"Three hours!? Are you crazy?"

To my surprise she turned to look at me like I was the crazy one and answered

"No, I'm not, we need the hours Eric, I THOUGHT we agreed on this beforehand." Giving me the stink eye and continuing saying "Besides, I feel like we haven't spent some alone time together in a while." she then looked at the floor and mumbled "I feel like I don't know you anymore." I looked at her and in a desperate attempt to get me to reconsider I guess, she squeezed my hand, looked up and pleaded "Pleasseeee....do it...for me." Giving me the puppy dog eyes as well. I groaned and caved to her demands by saying

"Oh alright you win. Three long boring hours it is."

We then took turns signing our name on this contract of some sorts to make it official which basically stated that we would be okay being watched by Officer Carter while we served our volunteering hours.

I felt like I was signing my life away.

Putting the finishing touches to our signatures, he took the contract away and dismissed us just like that and told us that we are excused for the rest of the day and to not worry about any makeup work for our classes as he'll "handle it". Part of me is really worried about what he means by that but I have bigger problems to worry about and that is how I or we are going to explain to the rest of the group our predicament. Hopefully the twelve other people that are thankfully still with us feel the same way and not leave too or else I don't know how I will ever get home.

Chapter 8

Good Samaritan

Thankfully our club members were supportive and understood the messy situation and promised us that they wouldn't do anything stupid to our rival club while we were gone. They also wished us luck and have fun as we deserve it for all of our efforts of keeping the club going. THAT'S A RELIEF. When it came time for us to go to this soup kitchen I was not looking forward to helping out whatsoever. Renée on the other hand was ecstatic. Reassuring me it would be fun and reminded me that we are killing two birds with one stone by regaining our respect, credibility as a club and helping the community. Touché, Touché.

I shrugged it off as we left the apartment to go meet with Officer Carter. Arriving at this soup kitchen we met Officer Carter who was waiting just outside the door for us and we walked inside together. The interior looked like your normal hospital waiting lounge of the 60s. Officer Carter then told us to sit down as I saw him put on this "act" and walked to the reception counter by tipping his hat and saying "Good afternoon Mam, I'm Sergeant Carter Briggs from New Orleans University where President Nolan notified your supervisor about the current situation of your volunteers today. I'll be outside just in case they pull anything during their scheduled time.

I overheard the receptionist reply "Why yes, I understand completely. I will let Christina know they are here and she will keep 'em busy. Thank you for letting us know Officer Carter, bye now." We then watched as he slowly walked out the door but not before making eye contact with both of us saying "I got my eyes on you two." before finally leaving. The moment he left, we heard the same female voice from behind say

"Oh hi there, you two must be the lucky helpers."

Renée and I turned around and there was this middle aged woman with short brown hair, brown eyes with average height and build in a dress walking in our direction.

"That's us!" Renée exclaimed, pointing at herself and me.

The woman looked over our shoulder and said "Thank goodness that pig left. He ain't the sharpest tool in the shed is he?" We all laughed acknowledging that was true. She continued saying "If he had one look at my name tag" pointing to it where it read:

Christina Wiggins – Director of Operations –

She then went on to say "I was the lucky lady talkin to that college President of yours and I am the person making sure this

soup kitchen is in tip toppy shape. Not some low level secretary"
She paused to cough and continued " Now if you two would be
eveh so kind and follow me, I'll show y'all where your stations
will be."

"Stations?" I asked concerned but Christina just laughed it
off saying

"Yes, here at St Mark's Soup Kitchen we believe everyone has
a special set of skills and your president told us how it would be
best for you two to do two different thangs. You'll see."

We were then guided through this door at the end of this
waiting room, the lady then gave us a little lecture about the
history of the soup kitchen and non profit. Right when she was
in the middle of this exciting story (take notice of my sarcasm
there) she suddenly stopped talking to comment "I am so glad
you two decided to volunteer here. We really appreciate it,
we usually don—I-I'm sorry, but I just noticed that beautiful
engagement ring. Congratulations to you two!" noticing Renée's
shiny gold engagement ring.

"Thank you." I replied, smiling down at Renée. "We're
excited."

"You two make a great couple. Now who's idea was it to come
and volunteer here?"

"It was hers." I said pointing at Renée, giving her the credit
and satisfaction.

"Of course it was." Christina said with a laugh. We were then
led to the kitchen which was hectic as there were a few cooks that

were already busy chopping vegetables and stirring pots and what appeared to be some humming and laughter coming from the few cooks that were there. I also took notice of the distinct aroma this kitchen had as it smelled like freshly cooked vegetables and broth. It was there that the kind lady introduced us to Head Chef Roberto and basically handed Renée off to him, stating how "Renée is going to be in the back here helping chop up some veggies and do some sweeping as she has a lot of experience or so I am told."

Anywho, once Renée got handed an apron and a hairnet, she was ordered by Roberto to get to work. As for me, Christina took me outside the kitchen that was far away from Renée to say "I got a very special job in mind for you Eric that very few volunteers get to do. Your going to meet our Chief Coordinator Benjamin where you are going to be helping him…along with our team by helping us with restocking some food for the food pantry and even get to help with some deliveries of home goods." clutching her hands and gasping with pure joy.

She introduced me to this Benjamin fella with his brown hair with a little gray to the sides and big 70s glasses, bell bottoms with a brown and red striped polo shirt while holding a clipboard as two guys were carrying a box from a truck. I was put to work right away after the introductions to him and the five workers were done. Heavy lifting is something I didn't plan on doing today and my body is totally going to regret that in the morning. Once we got all the boxes out of the semi-truck, we were then instructed to organize the food boxes by fruits and vegetables in two piles. The next step would be for us to "Take em out of these boxes, put them in the pantry and make them look like a christmas tree." or something like that as I recalled Benjamin saying.

Right when the other fellas were working on it, I was taking a breather wiping sweat from my forehead and that's when Benjamin pulled me aside saying How I deserve a break. Breathing a sigh of relief I was totally grateful that I wasn't going to be reprimanded for doing something wrong. That's when he mentioned that "We are goin on a little road trip...you and me. I'll explain on the way." He then told the other workers "Me and the new guy are going out for a couple deliveries and Christina will check on y'all progress while we're gone."

When we got outside the building, I saw this white van that read in big black letters :

St. Mark's Soup Kitchen on the side. Judging by my reaction and confused look, he clarified by stating that it was for "We gonna be doin some food deposits at some rough parts of the neighborhood." *Boy would I love to be in the kitchen cooking right now.* I thought to myself.

That never happened as Benjamin had ordered me to get in the van by opening the passenger door. I had no other choice but to hop in, he told me that we are making only three stops at some rough parts of the neighborhoods. It was not the kind where we are in some gang territory. Just the slums....you know the cheapest apartment that money can buy. Not the greatest but at least you have a roof over your head kind. At the first stop, looking at the cruddy apartment felt like I was in a cop show when they were busting someone for making drugs because that's what it looked like. We parked the car and he reassured me

"This is the place. We won't be long. In and Out. Here." handing me two paper grocery bags with handles with a white paper note stapled to the bag that read: ADDRESSED TO: Ms. Ashley Ward. Benjamin informed me that "Miss Ashley is one of our newest ones to be receiving our services. She's a new young single mother of two kids; twin boys that are a year old and she is just trying to make a living in this world like the rest of us."

"What of her folks…why didn't they take her in?" I asked.

I guess I asked the wrong question as he rubbed the back of his head and said "Son, the poor girl is only 18 years old and she doesn't even know who the daddy is and her parents kicked her out as she apparently "brought shame and bad luck" to her family." he gave a loud sigh and finished by stating "We do what we can at St. Mark's to help her and other women like her besides giving her groceries."

With four grocery bags in hand we walked toward the crusty and smelly apartment complex. We had to walk up two floors to get to her apartment number 215. Benjamin was the one who knocked on the door so we could be let in. After only a minute or two of waiting, the door slowly opened and out pops this young woman with a dress with a sunflower pattern, had blonde messy bed hair, runny makeup and had racoon eyes. Poor girl looked like she hadn't slept in days as she held her one year old with one hand who was wearing nothing but an Elmo diaper that was clearly soiled. Seeing the grateful face and smile of that young mother is what made my heart just stop. Before either of us said another word, she quietly reminded us as we walked in to "be careful where you step and do not talk so loud. I just got the other one sleeping not that long ago and he is in the other room."

HEARING THAT broke me. Like someone just ripped my heart out and stomped on it.

This apartment is no place for anyone to live. The place was filthy with clothes on the floor and chairs, the floors itself looked like they haven't been scrubbed in like a decade and don't get me started on the kitchen. We put the groceries on the only space available and that is the table where she profusely thanked us for the food. Before we left, she asked Benjamin if he could get her in contact with the support group which he nodded and told her to show up at the church office tomorrow around noon and they will go from there. After we were exited out of the apartment we didn't speak to each other until we got in the van when he told me that "We got two other deliveries, it's best if we keep on moving." I can tell he was deeply moved by what the girl said and didn't go into detail. The other two people we helped deliver food to were interesting to say the least. Like there was a kind but very senile old lady named Mrs. Beatrice Thompson who had several cats and her place smelled like it too. Finally the last person on our list was this one guy who had a few teeth and was wearing nothing but a wife beater and shorts. Also he smelled like he hadn't taken a shower or even touched a bar of soap for a month!

As Benjamin and I pulled up in the back lot of the Soup Kitchen, we made it back just in time for lunch. I was confused about...well everything. I mean why am I still here and what was the point in me tagging long when the fog can just put me in the sidelines and rest for a little bit before putting me back in the game so to speak. What lesson was there for me to learn?

I asked the only person I could trust with this question so I asked Renée as we were in line getting food

"What's the point in all of this?"

"It's about giving back to the community...Eric. There's nothing to it." she answered while mouthing a thank you to one of the lunch ladies handing out food.

"I'm sorry but how is this exactly giving back?" as the lunch lady plopped mashed potatoes and some greens on my plate along with a piece of chicken. Renée and I eyed a spot next to Christina Wiggins. As we slowly walked towards her and a few others that were at the table, I gestured to the homeless people who were sitting down at these cafeteria tables and added. "We are not changing their life...we are just prolonging it."

"It might not mean that much to **you**." Emphasizing on that last word. "But to these people." pointing at the people sitting around us. With her eyes now gazing at the floor then looking up "It means a whole lot." Renée paused for a moment and sat down next to Christina while I sat on the opposite end. I could tell that she was trying to get me to see the picture and added "Think of it this way, we are fortunate to have food on our plate, be with those that love us and most importantly have a roof over our heads." pointing to the ceiling "These people here don't have any of that and if we can just hand them food or give 'em a little bit of money, it makes a big difference in their life."

"She's right Eric. A little bit of kindness towards someone goes a long way." Christina jumped into our conversation to suggest that "Maybe God has put you in this situation to see what other good deeds you can accomplish besides being a good future husband, as Renée told me it was your idea coming here."

"Yeah…maybe." putting that comment in the far back of my head where I soon thanked her by saying

"Thanks, I try. It's been rough these past two weeks for us. I do what I can."

I don't know if it was the way I said it or sounded, but one glance at Renée and I could tell I had done something. As I watched her put her hand on her chest and let out a loving sigh. Where she then grabbed my hand tightly and said to Christina

"He has been the best fiancè-husband I could eveh dream of. He was there for me and my family when my big brotha died and when I was stressin about our school club, he knew the best way to distract me."

"What'd pretty boy do?" one of the women at our table asked as she was now intrigued by our conversation.

"Well I don't wanna brag, but he set up a surprise lunch date for me at my uncle's cafe." Renée playfully hit my shoulder, finished her bragging by exclaiming "Isn't he the sweetest?!"

"Sounds to me like he's a keeper." one of the women workers that were at our table remarked while others including Christina agreed.

"Why he sure is." Renée replied. Smiling gleefully.

Chapter 9

Close Encounter

Something about the way Renée said it, made me think I had given her mixed signals somehow. Whatever I did, Renée made a complete 180 degree turn in personality. When we finished our service hours and went back to our apartment so much was different.

I didn't think much about the change in Renée. I was even starting to like this new side of her more. All that changed after a few hours of us sitting together side by side watching what was now the Brady Bunch on our television set. During the end credits, she got up from the couch and told me that she will get started making dinner for the two of us. Even though my eyes were still glued to the tv, my mind wasn't so I replied "Okay. I'll be here still and holler if yuh need help with anything."

That was my first mistake as it took maybe five minutes tops of me watching what appeared to be Jeopardy. Now when I overheard her say to me that she's making Spaghetti and Meatballs tonight which according to her is Eric's favorite. She went on to explain to me that I apparently "deserved it, for all my hardwork recently." Renée then sweetly asks if I could head to the kitchen to "keep her company." Without thinking I got up from the couch, turned the tv off with the remote and did just that.

You see, when I saw her rolling the meat into little meatballs on the kitchen counter, I was impressed and said out loud

"Wow you did a great job."

"Well, what can I say....I am pretty good with my hands." she remarked. Me being me, joked

"Hey I am good with my hands too but I don't brag about it as much."

I've never seen her look so surprised and confused before. She even looked up and down at me before turning into hysterics and commented

"Oh that's funny, Eric." as she playfully hit my left shoulder and continued saying " I love you." ending it with a smooch on the cheek for a good couple of seconds. She wasn't done with me that easily yet as she walked behind me, smacking my tush in the process to add

"Seems like volunteering has put you in a good mood. Told yuh helpin out at the soup kitchen wouldn't be so bad."

"You're stealing my thunder." I had argued while playfully reciprocating that kiss.

"I don't know whatcha talkin bout." giving me the side eye. I knew she was only messing with me, so I replied

"Yes, you do. Going to the Soup Kitchen was my idea as to get Officer Carter off our backs."

"That may be true…bu-u-u-u-t-t-t" as she dragged that word and tried to get me to agree with her by stating "admit it, you enjoyed your time at the Soup Kitchen just as much as I did and wished we could've stayed there longer."

I stood there for a second or two thinking of it but I guess that was too long as Renée playfully threatened

"Don't make me tickle you for an answer Eric Striker. Cause you know I would." Without a second or two to lose I had no choice but to admit "Okay there's no need for that '' as I awkwardly laughed while putting her arms that were already in a tickling position down. I then tried but failed miserably to cover my laugh with a cough. I ended up admitting to her that "I-I-I know…I know. It's just that I wish…we had more moments like that. Makes it impossible with everything goin on." Unbeknownst to me, those were my final words of normalcy between us as a lightbulb idea seemed to have made a spark in Renée's head. The next thing I knew I heard her mumbling about going to the bathroom. I was weirded out as it was so sudden and bizzare but before leaving the kitchen she reminded me to "continue to roll the meat while I am gone. You're good at that." she snickered to herself , leaving me standing there in the kitchen while Renée was trying not to break into hysterics from her own joke.

God I love that woman.

....

Wait, no I don´t. That's a trick question. I–I ahh man why do I do this to myself?

She's cruel for playing with my err I mean Eric's emotions like that. That is so messed up.

When she finally came back into the kitchen I noticed that she had lighter clothing on. Not in color but seemed lighter and more loose somehow. I couldn't get a better look as I got distracted as she frowned and with her ruby lips curled said

"Heyyy you didn't finish rolling your meat." dragging that last word as she was now looking at the meat balls.

"Wouldn't be the first time." shrugging my shoulders.

"Ugh I can´t believe I am marrying such a manchild." rolling her eyes.

"You're the one that started all this meat humor, Renée not me."

"Yeah and I'm the one that fini-" she froze as she realized that she fell for her own dirty joke. I couldn't help it but ask with a raised eyebrow

"That what honey?"

She didn't answer, instead she just shook her head no. After a few seconds of silence, suddenly I hear her mutter "Nothing." then perked up saying "Let's get back to cooking." Once the meatballs were put in the pan to cook, the spaghetti was next on the list. As she was stirring the pot I noticed her white polo shirt looked particularly thin and I could see what appeared to be...pink underwear. I still didn't think anything was wrong or put two and two together so I sat down and began to have a nice peaceful dinner with her. This wasn't my first time sitting down with her to eat some good food in this apartment .

Looking back on it I was still oblivious to her messages and signals of something going down tonight. I even got myself ready for bed without batting an eye or noticing her signals which seemed to make her quite upset. Now there I was, casually brushing my teeth and when I just spit out the mouthwash dried myself with a towel, that's when I heard her voice call out in panic "Come quick Eric, I see something crawling up the wall. I think it's a spider!" I got out of the bathroom as quickly as I could and...WHAT THE HELL am I looking at?! *There's no spider or something climbing up the wall in the bedroom. It's only Renée sitting on the bed and....and looking all sexy like. Oh my goodness, what is she "almost" wearing?!* I thought to myself. I awkwardly tugged on my pajama shirt collar and said

"Wo-o-o-a-h-h-h-h! Renée what an outfit an– " before I could even finish my sentence she smiled weird, nodded fast and said

"This is all for you and this time it's in **PINK. Your Favorite.** You l-l-i-i-ike." dragging that last word with a creepy smile as she slowly started to pull down her left bra strap. Okay this is new. What do I do now? I guess I first gotta ask why she is wearing it?

"Uhh Renée, why are you wearing that?"

"I'm wearing it for you, silly." she answered giggling.

"For me?"

"Yeah, after all you decided to name MY brother Elijah as your best man, what you said to me back in the soup kitchen and not to mention that little date you set up just for me at my Uncle's Café was really sweet. So that got me thinking and I decided that you deserve a little treat tonight."

Oh I think "a little" is a bit of an understatement. I thought to myself. As she started to twirl a part of my pajama shirt around her finger, I kindly grabbed that finger and pulled her back where I told her that I have to go to the bathroom right now and I'll be right back.

" Promise?" she asked with her eyes looking like a hurt and lost puppy

"Pinky promise." as I shook my left pinky finger at her. I wish I could've just hightailed it out of there and never looked back but no, this crazy woman had the audacity to continue watching me like a hawk as I backtracked out the door where I had no choice but to head into our shared bathroom and close the door.

Being stuck in this 1960s blue marbled bathroom, I was a hot mess. I was pacing back and forth with so many questions and concerns. But mostly I was asking myself *Has she lost her mind?! Doing something like that to me! What has gotten into—oh no. No it can't be. She thinks I said this out of love and meant it too back at the cafeteria in the Soup Kitchen. Does every kind gesture men do result in this?* This bedroom banter between us has gone on long enough.....I want out. Maybe I can tell her nicely without breaking her heart. I then slowly opened the door and peeked through a little crack, saw her back turned to me and was kneeling on the bed patting herself down making her look irresistable.

I closed the door again and muttered "Nope. Can't do it. There's gotta be another way. *Ooo I know I'll climb out the window and escape through the fire escape ladder,* I thought to myself but as I made my way over to the window and opened it up carefully as I didn't want her to burst in and to my dismay, there was no fire escape ladder to the side or anything like that but there was a **Dumpster** with nothing in it to cushion my fall if I decided if a 12 foot drop was worth it. Seems like my idea of an escape route goes out the window just fine, instead of me. Great.....just....great. What do I do now?! Suddenly I hear a loud knock on the door. I was startled and with a lump in my throat I asked "Hello?" The person who scared me was Renée and I guess she was growing impatient with me and asked "Are you okay in there?" Sounding very concerned.

OH I WAS NOT OKAY WHATSOEVER.

BUT I WAS NOT COMFORTABLE TELLING HER THAT.

I ended up lying and instead told her that "Uhh yeah I am almost done." As I flushed the toilet and was now washing my hands. When she heard me washing my hands was the moment she believed me as I heard her footsteps leaving. I wish I could wash my hands forever but I knew better than to prolong my unfortunate situation.

Is this really how I am going to lose my V-card? To some crazy woman in 1970. Guess there's only one way to find out and I am afraid I won't like the aftermath. With that I turned the water off, dried my hands with a towel, and exited the bathroom. The moment I closed the door and turned around, I was surprised to see what Renée had done in the meantime. She was in the master bedroom still there kneeling on the bed as before but this time, the only lights in that room were the two lamps on our respective nightstands and the ceiling fan spinning.

Walking further into the room I started to hear some....some music playing in the background. Renée didn't waste another second as I watched her jump off the bed to slam the door behind me saying "It's time." Where I was then dragged by the arm to the bed. I stood frozen in fear with my back to the mattress, as she...she pushed me with both hands and I fell onto the bed. As I was staring at the ceiling fan, this crazy woman who was now on top of me, started to undress me. She first got rid of my nice blue striped buttoned pajama shirt with ease and chucked it across the room. Then came the pants.

I fought her tooth and nail on that one by squirming like a worm. Wasn't my smartest idea but it was better than kicking or slapping her. But somehow she mistook my squirming in fear for a horrible attempt to get my pants off faster and said "Stay still and let me help you." panting. "This will be over before you know it." The second I laid still hearing this, she took the opportunity to get them off of me and chucked them across the room too.

So there I was in bed, naked like the day I was born, with a woman…an attractive woman mind you, who is now on top of me pinning me down and flashing her breasts in my face as a way to…to..to get a reaction out of me. With each moan getting louder and louder. When that obviously failed, she didn't get the memo that I wasn't interested. Instead she bit her lip and said "Hmm this isn't working, let's try something else." While I on the other hand was a stuttering mess as I tried desperately to explain to her that I didn't want to do this but failed to even get a single word out. It was like my brain and mouth weren't communicating. The moment she let go of me, I immediately got up but she pulled me back down on the bed.

I had enough where I rolled her over, pinned her down on the bed and demanded that "This has got to stop." To my surprise she bit her lip, called my bluff and said "Why don't yuh make me. Tough guy. " Great, now she thinks we're role playing. To my surprise, she somehow broke free of my grasp, wrapped her arms around my neck and passionately kissed me on the lips. A good thirty seconds later it hit me of what she had done where I finally had gotten control of my––Eric's caveman urges. During our awkward spooning phase, Renée suddenly stopped.

To my shock and horror she began wiping sweat from her forehead and said almost out of breath "Looks like someone here wants it **rough.**" I could've easily broken free from her grasp but I was too tired and almost out of breath to even move a muscle. I know….I'm pathetic. Anyway, she then added while out of breath "Okayyy. Two can play that game, mistah." Then the spooning game was back on where we left off. She then giggled as she proclaimed "That's more like it. I think we are ready to take it up a notch." With a devilish grin she asked me

"You ready?"

"No" I managed to blurt out.

But just as she got closer down below and right when I thought I was about to sucker up and do the deed with her is when suddenly a loud crash that sounded like a car crash came right next to us by one of our windows. Renée must've seen what came through as she screamed in fear. In a panic, she sat up and pushed me off to the right side of the bed where I fell head first on the floor. I quickly got up and pretended that it was nothing when she; being in tears, begged me to check what was on the ground next to "our bed." I walked around to her side of the bed and saw that the window was clearly broken with glass shards on the floor. I then saw a good size of a gray rock just below the foot of the bed with a notebook paper attached to it. I ripped the paper off the brick and it threatened us in magazine cutout letters that read:

THIS IS THE FIRST OF MANY. STAY OUT OF OUR WAY. LEAVE AND NEVER COME BACK.

"I'm calling the police. Do not touch anything" as I quickly ran to the phone in the kitchen. I dialed 911 and explained a possible break in or vandalism. I gave the operator all the information she needed and reassured me that the police would be coming in a few minutes and to stay in the apartment. I thanked her and hung up where I calmly walked back to the master bedroom to find Renée still shaking from the experience where I told her that

The police should be here in a few minutes."

"Oh that's a relief. And Eric?" she asked.

"Yes." I answered

"Now might be a good time for you to put on some pants when you greet 'em at the door." as she tosses my pajama pants that she had chucked across the room.

Chapter 10

Aftermath

Police were no help in finding a culprit since the writing was in magazine cutout letters and whoever did throw the rock left in a hurry and according to them due to our... uhm..."unique situation" as they worded it, we couldn't have seen the perpetrator. So they had no choice but to close the case despite our clear and very vocal suggestions of it being Marcus and his gang. But our voices seemed to have fallen on deaf ears. Speaking of dead ends, Renée was distraught as this violence was hitting close to home. When the officers left she pulled my shirt to ask

"When will this end!?" as she wiped her tears from her eyes on my pajama shirt.

"I don't know Renée, hopefully soon." was all I could say as I comforted her. I guess it's safe to say her amorous mood was broken. Instead she told me that she would be the one sleeping on the couch.

"Funny, that's usually my thing" I silently joked to myself. She must've heard that as she angrily looked right at my soul and finger pointed at me, I knew I had screwed up.

"Now's not the time for jokes, love." she replied while yawning. I had no other choice but to back off. Fast forward to the next morning I don't know if Renée woke up on the wrong side of the bed or what but she began to be really snappy not just with me but to her other friends and family too for like the smallest of reasons. She even refused to hangout with her own friends on one occasion, no matter how much they begged. Soon it …was just me and her for a few days and would pull the pity "We are going to be married" card when I would go out with my friends without her. I don't mind spending alone time with the future Mrs. Striker but something is wrong. Very wrong.

Trying to change the mood, I announced that we are goin out to a local bar with friends as I "Am tired of stayin at home, doin nothin all day besides goin to school." Thankfully she agreed that a change of scenery would be nice. So it was settled. I immediately called all of our close friends to let them know my plan to help Renée come out of her comfort zone tonight. They all loved the idea and suggested going to this popular bar called Little Richie's Den, where according to them, Renée should be dancin and forget all about that broken window fiasco in no time.

We agreed to show up at Little Richie's Den but instead at 7:45 pm, I made sure that Renée and I were the first ones to arrive at the place a little earlier just so I can make her "loosen" up. I gotta say this place seemed to be quite lively with music playing and everybody was dancing and laughing….well everyone except Renée that is. Who looked sad as a kid who lost their balloon, sitting in a barstool next to me just twirling her green drink straw. "Come on Renée, have a good sip or two and loosen up will yuh." as I playfully nudged her left shoulder.

"Loosen up?" she asked as I saw her glaring daggers at me with one eye. She then better positioned herself to face me instead of the bar and continued saying "Last time I did that, a rock came through our window. I don't think anything can "loosen me up"." This is a start but I need something more.

Suddenly I heard You Don't Know Me by Ray Charles playing and I swear the whole room gasped with joy as the girls seemed to love this song and began dragging their partners to the dancefloor. I could tell Renée wanted to dance as I saw her get up then shake her head no and sit back down to finish her drink. BINGO. She just needs a little motivation…that's it! I casually turned to her and smoothly said

"Let's dance."

"What?" she asked as she turned to look at me in shock.

"Don't give me that look, I saw you get up." I paused as I pulled her out of that stool where I then said "Come on." as I began dragging her to the rest of the dancers despite her protests is when her mood entirely changed. She was acting like what the kids around here call "Groovy" and "Far out." But when we were dancing, something very strange happened. It was like those orange flashes I had before but only this time it was different. Like every twirl I gave to Renée, Emily Stewart; my actual girl-friend would appear with her blonde highlights wearing her spar-kling pink Homecoming dress, where she would smile, playfully laugh, and stare back at me with those sparkly brown eyes. By the fourth or fifth twirl I couldn't ignore it anymore where I had to stop dancing.

The moment I let go of whoever's hand I was grabbing, I swear I heard Emily's and Renée's voices merged together to ask "Is something wrong?" I rubbed my eyes and only saw Renée in her black dress with white ruffles having big round pearl earrings. "No, just uhh something got caught in my eye that's all. I think I got it." I quickly reassured her. *Whew! That was a close one.* Either I need to get my eyes checked or I think I had one too many drinks tonight because that was scary. I was pretty drained soon after that and I think Renée was too. So I led her back to the bar and that's when I heard this round of applause. In the distance I saw Dom, Owen, Patty, Sophie, Delilah, among a couple other people from our club with drinks already in their hands. Dom with a beer bottle that looked to be almost empty in his hand hollered as we walked over to them, "Wow that was quite the show. You two were pretty groovy out there." and Owen hollered soon after

"Hey Eric, save some of those far out dance moves for the rest of us. Huh" Everyone laughed while his girlfriend Sophie wrapped her arms around his chest smiling at us and commented

"You two looked terrific out there. Now it's our turn." as she seductively led the reluctant Owen to the dance floor. Don't worry Dom wasn't so lucky either. Renée, Delilah and the last two members of our club and I along with our redheaded friends named Angus and his irish twin Timmy laughed as we waved the lovebirds goodbye. When they were out of sight outta mind so to speak is when all of sudden from the far right corner of my eye saw someone dart towards us. When I say someone I mean Marcus who still looked like the Jimi Hendrix wannabe except for the fact his black scruffy beard he had was now just a pencil mustache. That's not all, he was now wearing a plain red headband around his forehead, a black leather vest with spikes on the side that looked something like bikers wear, a white t-shirt, bell bottoms, and black boots to complete his evil transformation. Oooo so scary! I am literally cowering in fear as we speak.

He He He.

"Well, well what a surprise to see you here." Marcus sarcastically announced.

"Well it is a pretty popular place." I replied.

Everyone turned to look at me annoyed...even Marcus.

"What!" I exclaimed "It is." with my hands up in the air as I turned to look back behind me.

Marcus who was trying to hold in his laughter said "Boy you never change Eric. Reminds me of the...the good ole days." He then paused, obviously reflecting back on them. Seems to me there is still some good left in Marcus. I can tell he was conflicted when talking to us as he definitely wanted to bring back the good ole days.

Maybe there's still a chance to save him before he is too far gone. But that was not the reason why he was here. Suddenly he went to reach something in his jacket's right pocket.Angus and Timmy stepped in front of us being the bodyguards. "Relax." Marcus reassured them and drew out a pack of Camel Cigarettes adding "Geez, can't let a man smoke in peace." He then lit a cig and put it in his mouth and puffed right in my face while saying "I want to talk to you two outside...alone." Marcus then looked at the two redheads and said "As you can see, I'm unarmed." as he opened his jacket, turned around to show them and us that we had nothing to fear. I was not buying it, he was planning something but Renée said "We'll meet you outside in a few minutes." he nodded and left. I was shocked, we all were.

"What was that for Renée?" one of the redheads asked.

"I think we can finally persuade Marcus to end this war with us."

"What makes you think he'll change his mind this time?" I asked as I wondered if our dancing had loosened some screws in her head.

"I know Marcus, he wouldn't try anything reckless or stupid. He sounded pretty serious."

"Okay."rolling my eyes I replied. "But if things go south Angus and Timmy won't be too far away." Luckily she agreed with me that we needed protection but from afar. Now as we went out by the back entrance looking around, Marcus was nowhere to be seen. I looked at Renée and told her

"I don't think Marcus is even he—"

Suddenly a punch came out of nowhere catching me right in the jaw. I went down on one knee as Marcus exclaimed "This is for calling my bluff." as he kicked me in the side as I tried to get up. Everything started to get blurry as I heard murmurs of what sounded like arguing between Renée and Marcus. I tried to get up but I was kicked again. This time in the stomach. Trying to get up while clutching my stomach I saw Marcus shoving Renée into the red brick wall. I don't know for sure what happened next. All I remember is ringing in my ears and Renée's voice pleading "Eric. What's gotten into you? Stop. You're hurting him, you're hurting him." I felt her trying to pull me away with the red hair twins helping to hold me back. In the next second I saw Marcus in front of me laying flat on his back on the pavement. Then all of a sudden I felt this weird jolt where I had this weird vision of Tommy Lee Cooper; the bad guy from my third adventure on the gymnasium floor with his black suit and when I looked down at my hands I saw I had a bloody knife. It felt so real that I could smell the blood too. It was still fresh in my mind.

I shook my head no and immediately let go of the tight fist I was making. I turned to her and asked "Are you alright? Are you hurt?"

"I think you're asking the wrong person." as she pointed to Marcus who was still on the ground. Then to my shock and horror she started to help the dude up even though he's the one that hurt me and her. Marcus groaned and I watched this beaten man wipe his bloody lip before getting up and said quite out of breath "Didn't know you could throw quite the punch."

"What can I say Marcus. I am full of surprises." He chuckled at that part and replied "Yeah, I almost forgot about it. Thanks for the reminder." He paused again to wipe the blood from his busted lip and added "Why don't we try to start things over....I have a little proposition for you two."

"Are you kidding me MARCUS! Not this again! That's what you wanted all along!"

"YES!" He exclaimed "Yes use that anger Renèe, you've been holding it inside for far too long." He then leaned closer to her and put both hands on her shoulders and said menacingly "Just let it all o-o-o-u-u-u t-t-t like your fiancé did." To my surprise she dropped her shoulders. Marcus proudly gave an evil smirk and said "G-o-o-o-d. Now join me, where you can use that held up anger on those who refuse to listen to our shared cause." I interjected by stating "That is not justice. That's you manipulating vulnerable people like Renée!"

He didn't like that one bit but he quickly turned his attention towards Renée as she looked uneasy and said "Renée, don't listen to the man. Besides me and you have history Renée. Doesn't that mean somethin to yuh? That history is what brought us togetha as close friends. Eric doesn't even know what it's like to lose a brotha! We do." He then took a long pause and said "STAND

WITH ME. Since we resolved our anger and frustrations with each other, why can't they!"

Renée's eyes went wide and actually looked very scared. I don't know if it was towards me or him as I guess Eric wasn't aware of what horrible secrets she had kept from him. I did the job for Eric by loudly asking "What does he mean by history... Renée?" all the while Marcus who gloated his little victory said "You neveh told him...he he he. I 'll leave yuh two be. Looks like you two need to have a long conversation." He gave a loud evil maniacal laugh before whistling and walking away like that whole fight never happened. Our fun night surely took some unexpected twists and turns.

The drive back to the apartment was short and quiet as I saved all my questions for when we were home alone. So when we got back to the apartment and just as I closed the door behind me I asked "Were you and Marcus ever a-a-a" "What? A couple?" Renée turned to ask me as she raised an eyebrow. "Oh just because I am a good person and helped, you get all roused up." she could tell I was still angry when she revealed to me that "You and I both know Marcus had it coming." pausing for a little while she said "He and I did have a history but it's not whatya think." I let out the breath I didn't even know I was holding. She continued to explain " We grew up on the same block togetha where he would walk me to and from school, hang out with me, Delilah and few other of our school friends occasionally but was always out with my brothers." She suddenly looked down at the floor and thought back "He lost a brotha too. Morgan Jacobs was his name and just turned 18 when he was forced to fight. He died on Marcus' 16th birthday back in '65. He and my brothers had been close ever since." She raised another eyebrow at me and asked "You seriously think my daddy allowed me to be with a boy all by myself." She shook her head at me in disappointment and stated "Look even if Marcus did "like" me, he never tried to have his way with me, he never gave me signals and even if he did, I never noticed or cared to do it back." Renée then muttered "You're my first and only boyfriend." Suddenly her anger came back full force as she stomped her foot, put her hands on her hips and steely stared down at me asking "What's your excuse for freakin out like that huh." With my hands out to her I simply said

"I'm just trying to protect you from bad apples, Renée, that's all. I don't want things to continue to turn violent for us. What would Eli think of this fighting?"

"What do you want to do instead, Einstein, continue to protest peacefully?" She argued

"I mean it worked with MLK." I answered.

"Yeah, until he got assassinated."

"That's not the point that I am trying to ma—"

"What is it?!" as she raised her voice to interrupt me. "What even is your point Eric? Cause up until now nothing has been working for us an–"

"I'm trying my best Renée, God I feel like I am the only one actually doing somethin here!" I yelled, reaching my boiling point. "If you can just shut up and let me speak my mi—" with anger in her eyes, I suddenly felt a hard slap across the right side of my face and looked at me with tears trickling down her face as she asked me "How **DARE** you. Talkin to me like I'm some sorta dummy! " She paused for a second to take a couple of deep breaths to calm down before she continued to rant "You didn't let me finish, Marcus was talkin…about my brotha…it's always been about my brotha! Him and Morgan had no other choice but to enlist and died because of it." Then with sniffles and watery eyes finished her rant by stating "That's what he was talkin about. Some history." She got choked up with her words and after a few seconds of silence she spoke clearly by reminding "me" that "You shoulda seen Eli's face when he got that rejection letter from that medical school in Florida. You think the first thing he wanted was to make my old man proud and go fight. Maybe you are the one who has forgotten…not me."

She paused to catch her breath and said "When I first brought you into my home, he was the only brotha that liked you a lot and hell for a big brotha, went out of his way and almost got in trouble just to make sure all the fellas in our hood KNEW that you weren't worth messin with." She then grabbed my shirt and with tears added "He wanted to be a doctor, Eric. A doctor. Not taking lives but saving them." She sighed, recalling something from memory then angrily shouts "It's his fault he got cocky by not applyin to more schools then maybe he would still be here breathin and laughin." Tearing up she in a low voice admitted

101

"But he ain't." Wiping a tear from her left eye with some sniffles and continued "Before he left to go fight, he told me that he sees himself in you. Now you tell me Einstein, what he means by that or you keep this stupid ring." as she took the ring off her finger and held it in front of me.

She then ended her rant with "I'm serious." she put the ring back on her finger, let go of my shirt and pushed me away. To go think it over. I could tell she was deadly serious. Considering long and hard what she said about calling off a wedding, I knew this was pretty important. If I fail here, my Lucas brain tells me that Eric and Renée will never get back together. I guess I have no other choice but to wing it. Here goes nothin.

"Renée, you know I am no mind reader."

"What are you then? A fortune teller?" She rudely snapped back at me to ask.

"No, but I do know how much Eli means to you. You loved him more than anyone, even me and was your rock. He knew it too." I stopped abruptly. I suddenly got a bright idea on how to save this relationship, it's ballsy but it might work.

"He was your rock just as you were to him, you eveh think how much it hurt him. Knowing he probably won't make it back, I was there comfortin him, the same way I did to you when he passed away." She was about to say something but I quickly added "What about when our window smashed with that note at our place a while ago, I was there holdin your hand as the pigs interviewed you. He may have been the biggest rock in the world but I was there to hold him together at the end and that's what I am tryin to do with you right now."

She was speechless. Renée's face went through a series of emotions from crying to happy to angry. I knew she was emotionally vulnerable but it was no use reasoning with her. Marcus had gotten into her head as she began to talk crazy like "Maybe we are doing this protesting all wrong. Maybe Marcus is right" I interrupted her saying "Renée, stop for a second and listen to yourself, you're starting to sound like him. YOUR SCARING ME. Is that what you really want to be like?"

"You know what, Eric. I do, I really do. Since violence cannot bring Eli or Morgan back, maybe causing some violence here and there is the only way to get people's attention on what matters." My eyes went wide and just stammered "W-W-Wait Renée, stop and think about this don't let yourself get carried aw—" Renée, who looked like she might break a vein in her forehead suddenly shouted "I'm tired of thinkin! Alright! I'm joining him. I've already made up my mind and there's nothing you can do to stop me." She slammed the front door of our apartment on her way out.

Chapter 11

Distraction

A week has gone by since Renée's sudden betrayal and I still feel like my heart got ripped in two. I didn't even want to sleep in the same bed after our argument. I slept on the couch. After that night, I decided to couch surf with Eric's buddies who were more than willing to help me out. If this is how people feel after a breakup...then leave me out of it. It's the worst feeling in the world. I would pay someone serious money to make sure I will never experience this ever again.

I retreated into hermit mode. Nothing and I mean nothing seemed to get me out of this hermit like state. Renée's friends who luckily totally understood my feelings tried to help. In fact it actually made it worse as it was not the same without Renée being there. It wasn't until Eric's good buddy Randy decided it might be a good idea to try and cheer me up by taking me bar hopping. His good intentions couldn't break through my unhappiness.

Every single girl I met with their beautiful eyelashes, suggestive glances, had left me with a sour taste in my mouth.

In my clouded judgment I did the unthinkable and contacted Renée that night when we were back at Randy's place. All the guys tried to discourage me from doing it, but I didn't listen. I should've and immediately regretted my decision. Luckily I had enough presence of mind to not reveal anything about my true self or the fog. I told her my laundry list of grievances but all she seemed to care about was me apologizing for my actions and joining Marcus´ side which according to her is the right way of taking care of business.

Well I decided to stand my ground as my belief still works and stands. Killing or hurting doesn't solve problems. It prolongs them. Next morning, still recovering from a horrible hangover, the teal dial phone across the room started ringing. It felt like a brass band marching through my head. I let it continue to ring until Randy finally went over to pick up the call. It sounded like he knew whoever was on the other end as I overheard him saying "Yeah, I´ll get him." He then put one hand over the phone and hollered for me and said that "It's one of Renée´s brothers on the phone and wants to speak to you ." Feeling there was nothing to lose at this point, I took the receiver from Randy and groggigly said "Yeahhhhh" into the phone.

"Eric, It's me Roger, I tried calling Renée but she said she is busy and said to bother you instead. Sayin something about you sleeping over at a friend's place? What's that about…did yuh have a fight?" I then heard him cough awkwardly when I didn't answer so to break some tension he switched topics by asking "Do you remember you sayin that you'll make time out of your day for me."

"Uhm....yeah what about it?" I answered, recalling what I had said to him back at Renée's parents place.

"We-e-l-l-l-l, one of my last football practices as a junior is tomorrow and both my parents are workin and can't watch me practice but will be there for the game. Since Irving and Renée can't make it, I was wonderin if you can watch me play." I was silent as a mouse as he then explained trying to hold it together "That's what Elijah did before...before he-he-he got drafted and it would really mean alot to me if you could stay and watch even if it's for a minute or two."

"What time does it start?"

"3:30 right after school."

"I'll see what I can do but I can't make any promises that I will be there for sure. I gotta go. Bye" and hung up the phone.

"Who was that?" asked Dom as he walked in the living room.

"That was Roger, Renée's little brother and he was asking if I could show up to his football practice."

"What'd you say?"

"I told him, I would think about it."

"Think about it!" Dom exclaimed. "No thinking, you're goin. You need to clear your head man."

Maybe Dom was right about clearing my head as I did end up going. When the time came as I stared at my brown leather watch, it wasn't hard finding the highschool that Rodge went to as "East Clover High School" that I now recall seeing when me and René passed by when we were on our way to visit the Bowman family for the Saints game had to be the one he goes to. Anyway, I found a good parking spot behind the bleachers and easily hopped over the black metal fence and casually strolled to find a good spot to see the players practice for their upcoming game..

They were doing pretty good but the MVP of this little practice game was number 72 who was this amazing wide receiver. Boy, could that kid could run. When he scored a touchdown, I couldn't help but stand up, cheer and whistle while he celebrated. Everyone on and off the field immediately turned around to look at me. I was totally embarrassed by my outburst and sat down. To my surprise one of the highschool coaches who recognized me, I guess, shouted "I see someone is keeping the tradition alive. Come down here son. The bench has a much better view."

I didn't question it, made my way down the stadium steps, walked to this gate and there I was on the football field. Wow! The two coaches who were there patted me on the back, along with the other players like I was a celebrity or something. Suddenly I heard someone say "You came. You Really CAME! I don't believe it." I turned around and wide receiver number 72 took off his helmet and gave me a bear hug. That's when it finally clicked that the talented wide receiver kid I was watching and admired earlier was Roger.

Wow! I gotta say I hope he has a scholarship or something lined up in the future. He's a natural. I noticed he looked over my shoulder while hugging me and stopped to ask if his sister was with me. I awkwardly told him that she couldn't make it. Before he could continue, the same coach hollered at us to "Stop talking Ladies and hussle over here! Move! Move!" We did as instructed and made our way to the benches, one of the coaches told me to stand with them as I had "earned it."

Whatever that means. The head coach I guess introduced me to the team as I was apparently a "star athlete" quarterback in highschool before a career ending ACL tear on my right leg ruined my chances to "be somebody". He even gave me the opportunity to say something motivational to their team for the big game against their sworn enemies "The Tigers." tomorrow.

No problem, right. Wrong! I was not ready. So I gulped and nervously said "I-I don't know what to say other than thanks Coach." I coughed and continued "You guys are going to need more than a lousy heartfelt speech to take on the tigers. This is speaking from experience. All yall are brothers, it doesn't matter the color of your skin or some other thing. On the field you are all the same, tigers don't go in groups and neither should ya'll." I took a deep breath and added, "But I promise you, if you work and communicate with each other, you'll beat them so badly they'll have to rename their team to "The Kittens." Everyone laughed at that one. Where one of the football players said "You heard the man, we got this!" Then to my surprise they, without saying a word, put their hands in the middle, and told me to do the same. They then said this cheesy football chant and ended it with "Gooo Mustangs!" Hopefully that will get them riled up for tomorrow.

I am no motivational speaker but I like to think I did a good job. The football players seemed to love it. Even Roger. I watched from the bench for the next half hour or so till practice broke up and everyone got to go home. I waited outside of the men's locker room when Rodge went in with the rest of the guys. I wanted to say how proud I was of his performance before I had to leave.

At the end of practice Roger was like a little kid seeking approval by asking "Did you see any Scouts watchin us practice, Eric?" I didn't answer. Sensing the awkward tension, he changed topics by pointing out

"It's Renèe isn't it?"

"Huh?"

"She's the one who got under your skin."

"Yeah, what gave it away?"

"All women like to push our buttons. Renée ain't different." I looked at him surprised as I was not expecting him to say that.

"Man, you're pretty observant for your age"

"Thanks. Runs in the family. So about my sistah, she'll come around, don't worry. She always does. You did a good thing by giving her space."

Walking across the school parking lot together, he acted all high and mighty with how good he is and asked me "Anyway, now that you finally saw my moves, you want to see the look on The Tiger's faces when we beat 'em tomorrow night."

"Hell yeah, I am in. The game starts at 6 right?" He nodded. "Well this is goodbye I guess." As I waved goodbye to Roger , I took only five steps away from him when he awkwardly hollered

"Hey Eric?"

I slowly turned around and wondered *What could he possibly want now?*

"Can I ride with you?" he asked, giving me the pleading eyes and puffed his lips out. To really sell it. "Why?" I asked, annoyed. "Your legs don't work anymore."

I may have found that amusing but Roger gave me the annoyed look and stated "I just saw my buddies leave without me." He then made this pouty face but if I knew teenage boys, which I do, I knew there was more behind what he was saying. With that I asked him "Because?" as I gestured to him to keep talking. "Cause-Cause I may have already told 'em you would drop me off home." He laughed awkwardly and smiled goofy. I loudly groaned and said "Okay you can ride with me kid."

"Sweet! Thanks Brotha, I owe yuh one!" he replied. I let him continue walking as it's been too long since I got to experience being an older brother again. I then hollered "Hey Rodge." He turned around and the look of embarrassment will forever be ingrained in my head as I told him that "My van is actually that way."

Pointing to the back of the stadium. "Oh." I heard him mutter and backpedaled. We then walked together, making jokes and busting each other's chops along the way. This is the first time in ages where I felt like I was a big brother again and it felt good.

Really good, almost felt like I shouldn't embarrass him. Almost. The moment I parked the van in the driveway, Roger hopped out and immediately ran to the front door and rang the doorbell with me standing a good couple feet away. Renée's mother opens the door and before she even says a word, Roger brushes right past her like she was a ghost. She then says "Kids these days." as she looked behind her and shook her head. She then clasped her hands and said "Ah! Eric! What a surprise seeing you so unexpected. Come in...come in." ushering me inside. The moment I take my first steps inside, she shuts the door behind me and pulls me aside and says "Thank you for showin up at Roger's practice today. It really means a lot not just to him but to us too. I tried to be there for him today but-but. Sorry." putting a hand out and wiping her tears with her other arm.

"He was just askin and askin, and I had to go to work and—"

"Momma, I'm positive Roger didn't take it personally. If he did, you know you would be the first one I would talk to yuh about. You're a good mother." She breathed a sigh, patted my shoulder, looked me dead in the eyes saying "And you're a good son. I hope you know that." Then like a switch she was back to her perky self. So that's where Renée gets that from. Speaking of Renée, I was afraid she'll bring her up and I was right. We were sitting at the kitchen table talking as it was only the three of us in the house as Irving had to go take the night shift and Renée's dad was still working down at the docks. While sipping her glass of coke she asked me "I was surprised to only see you at the door. Usually you and my baby gal can't go one day without each other."

"She couldn't make it, she was busy."

Renée's mother put the drink down on the table and shook her head saying

"Child, I know my own daughter to know that whatcha said to me ain't true. What is it?"

Dang, she is good. Without having any other choice, I explained that we had a major fight a week ago over Elijah and how my way is the right way of seeking justice and how she is stubborn to not drop it. She sighed and said "That's my baby gal for yuh. Call it mother's intuition but I have a funny feelin she'll come poundin on your front door soon, beggin for forgiveness." I hope she's right. It was time for me to leave and as she walked me out she said "I better go on to reminding a certain someone in this house to take a shower. I hope to see yuh at Roger's game tomorrow." Smiling, I walked out feeling satisfied that today turned out better than expected.

I met with Renée's family at the big game the following day and it was nice to see all of them in the stands cheering when I saw the East Clover High football team run onto the field. Most everyone seemed glad to see. I spotted Renée with her afro,

113

blue senior varsity jacket with the numbers 63 on the left side. I recognized that as Eli´s varsity jacket and she was wearing these black tights with a plain blue skirt and black shoes, standing with her family. Taking a deep breath, I walked up the bleachers where I asked if this seat was taken. They turned as one and said "Sit here." Except for Renée. She being the dead beat downer looked coldy at me and said "Sit somewhere else." Irving poked her shoulder saying "Be Nice."

She of course groaned and scooted closer to her brother giving me some room to sit down. I wish Renée also took her brother ´s advice as she made it her mission to annoy or at the very least, get me to sit as far away from her and her family as humanly possible. It just kept on getting worse and worse until someone right next to us shouted "That's it, I had enough of this!" We turned to see who shouted that and it was Renée´s mother who had whipped her head 180 degrees in our direction and stated "You two are no longer welcome sitting here with us until this fight of yours is settled or on pause. Do yuh understand me?" "Yes Ma´m." We grudgingly answered in unison. We both got up, left the stands and walked to where no one could hear us. Continuing our argument for a few more minutes, I stopped abruptly turned to face her and said

"What are we doing?"

"What are we doin? I'll tell yuh wh—"

"That's not what I meant." I interrupted to point out. "What I meant is fighting. We are letting this lousy argument get the best of us and it's ruining the reason why we are here in the first place. We came here to support your brother Roger Bowman right? Do you care more about us fighting than supporting him?"

"Of course not. I care. What kind of question is that? I love my little brotha to bits."

"Good, I do too, so let's agree right now to put our little fight on hold and go watch Roger."

"For Roger." she muttered. Finally we agreed on something. We walked back to the bleachers and found a spot not too far away from her family where we can have a little bit of privacy. She took a seat and I sat in the row behind and above her. It took a while but she got comfortable right when halftime was over. Where throughout the rest of the game I took my attention away from the game, spotted her not below anymore but right next to me, making herself at home by having my arm across her shoulder.

Soon it turned into a tight squeeze on my right hand where we both saw Roger get a nasty tackle while running with the ball trying to get a touchdown. He didn't get up right away where I squeezed her hand, told her that he's gonna be alright as he's one tough kid. There were moments where I honestly forgot what we were even fighting about in the first place and I think Renée did too. I know for a fact she felt cozy as she was snuggling in my arms.

Unfortunately the feeling didn't last. As soon as the game was over we all complimented and congratulated Roger on their

115

team's victory over their rival school. Exiting the stadium with her family, I followed them but as I watched Renée get ready to get in her family's Ford 1950s dark green station wagon, she turned to say "Thanks for being with us at the game…but that doesn't mean anything. Our fight ain't over. I still haven't fully forgiven you about what you said about me." She then whipped her head back around and got in the family car. Awkwardly standing there, everyone around me seemed to walk through me. I felt like a ghost.

Chapter 12

Renée

The next part of my story is actually going to be told by someone else for a change and it's Renée Bowman herself. I see you looking to the side of my hallway like some desperate paparazzi...she's not there. I'm sorry to disappoint you but she is not coming in person as I never told her or anyone in my adventures through time who I really was. Instead I am going to show you a video clip that I found on Youtube just a year after my crazy adventure through time had officially ended. This interview was taken a week after I had left Eric Striker's life for good to give you some context. So without further ado, here's a snippet of the two hour-long interview of what happened immediately after Renèe left me standing there at the school parking lot.

So kick back, have a drink, grab some popcorn even, and enjoy the show.

Hits play

Interviewer: Do you feel sorry for leaving your fiancé in the parking lot?

Renée (frustrated): At the time, no not really. I thought he deserved it. (The interviewer was flabbergasted by this but before he could say another word Renée quickly said:) Words can hurt. (He silently nodded.) Good, now Peter, what he said to me back then did hurt but not anymore.We talked it out.

Interviewer: Do you still believe that what he said was just him as you put it "Havin one of 'em strange moments?"

Renée: Eric may have been actin a little strange but those three weeks after my big brother died, made everyone a lil strange.

Interviewer (Seen stroking his black beard): Hmmm, good point.

Renée: Being without Eric for the first day was tough. It really was. But he was right, Marcus was a manipulator.

Interviewer: For the viewers out there watching this at home, can you describe in detail how Marcus was exactly manipulating you so others won't fall victim?

Renée: H-He was my friend. I thought he was, but when he came to pick me up from my parents' house, things were normal but when we were far away from my folks, he started yellin at me. He's never done this to me before. While my other friend Jermey who was in the backseat just sat by and did absolutely nothin except egg him on. (throws her hands in the air)

Interviewer: What did Marcus exactly say to you?

Renée: H-H-e-e-e first asked me if I had a good time cuddlin with my future hubby in the bleachers? At first I was like uhh what? So I lied and told them that I was nowhere near Eric. Even though I was and enjoyed every minute. They of course didn't buy it as Marcus added "Cut the bull-talk, Renée we saw you. "

"What?! No you di—" before I could finish speaking, Jermey pulled out a pair of black binoculars out of thin air and proceeded to wave them at my face. I was speechless.

Interviewer (suddenly pulls his chair closer to Renée and with a stone cold look on his face asks): Are you aware of the "Peeping Tom" Act? (Renée shakes her head no.) According to Louisiana law, First time offenders who spy on others without their consent have a $600 fine for first time offenders and could also add additional sentencing to Marcus' charges.

Renée (Smirks): Thanks for lettin me know. I'll talk to my lawyer and see what we can do about it after this interview talk is over. Where was I?

Interviewer: The Binoculars in Jermey's hands.

Renée: Right. So he has 'em binoculars right and says to me "We saw you with this bad boy." while giving a toothy grin. I remember screaming my head off at both of them like "You were out here in the parkin lot spyin on me?! How could yo—"

That's when Marcus returned the favor by screaming at me "Of course we did! You think we would fully trust someone new to this group who has only been with us for a week with all of our little secrets." He then slowly stroked my cheek which was dripping with tears and said "You gotta remember that this ain't your club Renèe. So I suggest you get used to my style fast or we might have some problems you dig" he then sighed and put one hand on my shoulder and added "I only did it for your protection Renée as we don't fully trust

you yet. It's nothin personal."

Jermey added "Yeah we don´t trust you yet, don't take it so personally and did you tell your sweet hubby anythang about our project."

With a blank stare told them " I didn't tell him a thing."

"Good. Make sure it stays that way." Marcus replied.

Interviewer: What were their plans for this project?

Renée (seen rolling her eyes in annoyance) : I was gettin to that. Geez. They didn't let me know what it was when I first joined other than it was top secret. I didn't know at the time but I was the getaway driver for their group activities. I saw them come back to the van one time where they were wearing ski masks and looked like they got the stuffing knocked out of them as they were all running towards me looking bloody and bruised, especially Marcus.

Interviewer: Did you question it?

Renée: No. I was too stunned. They never told me anythang except where to go, turn and lay low for a while. I didn't see anything or knew where I was at times. But what I do know is that what I did was enough to earn their trust as the following day, I was brought to this abandoned warehouse in the city. According to Marcus, this was the perfect hideout. The Warehouse had not been used since WWII where no one, not even Eric would think we were hiding. As he opened the metal door to this place, I was surprised to see a production line of people or as Marcus had put it, members of our group who gladly "Volunteered".

Interviewer: What were these "Volunteers" creating exactly?

Renée: They weren't making arts and crafts okay! These so-called members of his group were assembling weapons to do some serious damage. As each weapon was finished, it was being placed at the end of the long brown assembly table. The pile was growing. Noticing me looking in that direction, Marcus informed me that he got in contact with his Uncle who was a Gun Smuggler in Africa during WWII and through him he was able to get a good amount of weapons.

Interviewer (looking intrigued): What kind of weapons?

Renée (agitated): Ak47s, revolvers, and just for the fun of it, he happily told and showed me that his Uncle surprised him with a bazooka to start out his club with a "bang" and Marcus even bragged about gettin that bazooka as if it was an early birthday present.

Interviewer (eyes wide and adjusts his glasses): Seems to me with that kind of arsenal, Marcus could've started another war.

Renée: More like a **Revolution** as he happily referred to it. (There was a few seconds before Renèe had spoken again and this time she looked ashamed as she started to say:)

121

I was uncomfortable seeing all these weapons and felt like I wanted to run outside and puke. But my good ole friend Marcus reassured me that "We'll only be using 'em for self defense or as a last resort." Suddenly my tour was cut short as someone walked up to him to whisper in his ear that someone wanted to speak with him privately in his office. Hearing this, Marcus then turned to look at me and said "We can continue the tour some other time Renèe, I gotta go. This is important. But you just have fun and explore for a bit, this shouldn't take long." I watched him walk a flight of metal stairs to this office space that was up above the assembly room floor. It reminded me more of a watchtower than an office. As there was someone up there pacing back and forth watching what was going on below. Suddenly two bodyguards who came from thin air bumped my shoulder as they walked up those steps so fast that they were now right behind Marcus. Leaving me to wander through the area alone.

Interviewer: What did you end up doing before Marcus came back for you?

Renée: Explore. What else? (as if it was a joke.) I looked around and this place was sooo big. I know it's a warehouse but I've never been inside one before. Anyway while explorin, I found two guards in plaid shirts and jeans with AK's strapped behind their back and standing next to each other appearing to guard a brown door. As I walked closer, I heard noises.

Interviewer: Construction?

Renée: No. I heard ticking and people talking in another language from whatever was behind that Door!

Interviewer (casts shade of doubt): Ticking?

Renèe: Yes, ticking like that of an alarm clock and people whose voices don't sound familiar. I tried to see past the guards but as soon as I got closer.....I was spotted. The guards I recognized as Dylan and Will from my "former" group pointed their guns at my face. I raised my hands up and said "Dill, Will, you know me. Put the guns down."

The guards looked at each other and did as I suggested and replied "Sorry Renée, we're under strict orders by Marcus to not let anyone besides him and Huan through this door."

"Huan? He's here?!"

"Mhmm. Now you better high tail it outta here, if you know what's good for yuh." Dylan had replied.

Interviewer: Who exactly is Huan? Is he a friend of yours?

Renée (groaned): Peter, haven't you heard the new news that Huan Su Ming is one of the smartest kids on our campus and he had been missing along with a ragtag team of top engineering students for 2 weeks. Police found no evidence of a struggle or anything.

Interviewer: Oh, him. Now I do, sorry. Marcus sounds like one smart man.

Renèe: And that is my worry that still keeps me up at night. If he's smart enough to stump and evade the police, what about the trial coming up?

Interviewer: Renèe you're doing it again. There's nothing to fear. Marcus is being held in the most serious solitary confinement holding cell in the state of Louisiana. Now let's get back on track. So Whatd yuh…(coughs) what did you do after Dill said that to you.

Renèe: I left the area as Marcus neveh said anything about Huan since I've been here. And if I know Marcus, he would like it to keep it that way. It was a good thing I was far away from that door as Marcus came running toward me and looking frantic, asking "Have you been through that door?" I lied and asked him "What door?" He looked at me for a few seconds and answered "Here, I'll show you. He signaled for me to follow him and I was getting nervous as we slowly walked to the door. My heart was pounding and a million thoughts and worries were going through my mind like *What if those two guards would tell him that I was just here when I told Marcus I wasn't or even knew there was a door here.*

Luckily for me there was no one guarding the door this time. Marcus, ready to use his key, told me "When we go in, you don't say a word to anybody, you dig?" I slowly nodded my head.

"Good." he opened the door and held it with a smile saying "Ladies first."

I walked in and…and…and.

Interviewer: And what? What'd you see?

Renèe (eyes watery): Can I have a tissue?

(Someone from off camera hands her a tissue and then says:) Thanks (as she wipes her eyes then blows her nose before going back to her story) It was horrible, oh so horrible. There were a dozen dirty men that I actually recognized as people who went to school with us. I don't know them by name exactly but I know they were people like Huan. Smart engineering students who were on top of their classes who strangely disappeared without a trace a few days before Huan did. Eric and I never gave their absence a second thought because it's college and people drop out or transfer suddenly. It happens all the time.

Now here were the missing students in this small room with a brown wooden workbench, papers everywhere, a chalkboard in a corner with some charts and a pictured design that looked like some sort of button control device. Whatever it was, it had been really obscured. The students looked disheveled and as if they hadn't slept in days, they looked like they were being worked... to death.

Interviewer: Did you tell Marcus what you noticed?

Renèe: No. Marcus lied and said our "special volunteers" are working day and night to create some special effects for when we make our grand entrance this Saturday.

Interviewer: Did you buy that?

Renèe: Oh Hell-heck no! Not in the slightest as not even once of his rambling did he mention Huan and that made me suspicious of what he was really planning, probably not some innocent special effects. Abruptly Marcus' demeanor changed and I was instantly no longer welcomed and was hurriedly ushered out of the building. I wasn't satisfied, I wanted more answers.

Interviewer: What did you do?

Renèe: I wanted proof of what was being planned so there would be no secrets being held from me. Unfortunately I didn't get to use my camera (Showing a Poloroid model 95 to the Interviewer. She then puts it on her lap and adds:) So people like Eric will believe me. Interviewer (smirking and nodding his head before asking): Did you go back the same day to take the photos?

Renèe: No, I had to be sure I had Marcus' trust. Surprisingly later the same day, Marcus stopped by at my parent's house, and handed me a spare key to the backroom telling me to guard it or not let it fall into the wrong hands.

Interviewer: So you went to take the photos tomorrow not on the same day. Is my assumption correct?

Renèe: Yeah, that's about right. I went tomorrow afternoon as I knew Marcus and the guards had class so I had about three hours, maybe even less than that to take pictures, without being undetected, making too much of a mess and getting out.

Interviewer: And you didn't go to Eric…. because? (Leading her on for an explanation)

Renèe (looking sheepish): I'm not perfect okay. Nobody is. I thought there's gotta be a good excuse for Marcus being the way he is. Besides, if I cave in and go to Eric then I'm afraid he wouldn't believe me. I needed to prove not just to myself but to other women too that I don't need a man's help every time something serious happens that I can handle it on my own.

Interviewer: Very Inspiring. So please tell the people at home how you managed to get the photos.

Renèe: It was harder than it looked. Putting aside my uncertainty, I pulled up to the place and even hid my car behind a large bush as a precaution.

Interviewer: Good call Renèe. How'd you get inside? Through a window, front door, and were there any alarms?

Renèe: I went through an open window as the door was locked. From there I took pictures of all the different areas as you can tell.

Interviewer: Did you meet these so-called "volunteers"

Renèe: I tried but only one spoke English while the rest were actually foreign exchange students who spoke Chinese and German. The one English speaker who was fluent in both languages told me that they've been held here against their will for two weeks and since none of the other students here spoke english; Marcus kidnapped someone who spoke both languages was Huan Su Ming and he's held in a shed out back. He then demanded that I release them. I told him to tell the others that I couldn't do it yet as I'm here to make sure Marcus goes to jail for good but I would be back for them. (She coughs)

Interviewer: Interesting. Then what happened?

Renèe: They all gratefully wished me luck but before I left, the kid told me that Huan left the blueprint for the " special effects" upstairs in Marcus´ office and that is the key to stopping Marcus.

I left and locked up and quickly headed up the long flights of stairs to his office.

Interviewer: Was the office space booby trapped?

Renèe: I was wondering that too, but the front door was surprisingly unlocked so I walked right in. I had to go on my hands and feet almost. So no one saw me from the window which was overlooking the entire inside of the building. I found the blueprint where he said it would be and took some pretty good photos that LIFE Magazine might hire me. (Laughs to herself) But just as I took a close up shot of the blueprint, that's when I heard voices and footsteps coming my way.

Interviewer: Did you recognize them?

Renèe: Yeah it was Huan Su Ming and Marcus.

Interviewer (looking surprised): I thought you said he was at school.

Renèe: Well apparently class ended early that day. So I ran and hid inside of a big wardrobe closet that was in his office. The moment I closed the closest door fully I heard Marcus shout "HUAN!" As he opened the front of the door

"I thought I told yuh to keep this door locked. Don't want any Peepin Tom´s spyin on us.

" You're worried for nothing, Marcus. No one knows we are here…or what we are doing."

Their conversations got pretty muffled as they walked further away from the closet in the big office. But I did overhear Huan and Marcus continue arguing as Huan said something about

"Progress" and "Explosives"

Whatever progress they made, didn't satisfy Marcus as he grumbled "That's not good enough Huan. We need more than just one bomb. We need three to start our very own Revolution with a bang."

Interviewer (surprised): Are you one hundred percent certain that is what you heard him say? Do you plan on testifying in court when the trial does come?

Renée: Yes, hearing and seeing explosives for the first time is something you never forget. Can I continue? Or are you going to keep interruptin me?

Interviewer: No. Carry on.

Renée: Anyway, I peeked the closet door a little and saw how upset Huan was and watched him burst a gasket by loudly complaining "But Marcus, the men that gladly "volunteered" for your cause are starving and we don't have enough food or even the supplies necessary to meet yo—"

Marcus had enough of his yappin and smacked him in the head that made Huan head spin like a top. I gasped but held my mouth shut with one hand and heard Marcus barking

"That's enough outta you." hitting Huan one more time for good measure. "Leave the supplies, food and volunteers to me. We got a schedule to keep. Now move." As I watched him hit Huan in the back with his rifle with such force. It still makes me sick to my stomach. And to think this was the sweet little boy that used to live on my block and walk me to school. (she takes a deep breath and continues onward stating:)

Renée: When those two eventually left, I came out of the closet and took a good photo of the blueprint of the one bomb they conveniently left on the desk with this Poloroid (Showing a Poloroid model 95 to the Interviewer. Where she then puts it below her seat, states:)

Renée: I had to sneak my way out of the office without being noticed so I watched those two walk to the backroom where the "volunteers" were held and escaped through the same window I came from which wasn't easy. Believe me. Once I was free and a good distance away, I hopped in my car and sped like never before.

Interviewer: Are there any final thoughts you had before making that decision?

Renèe: The only thought I had at the time was

A Bomb?!

Okay Marcus has gotten too far. I remember thinking to myself. *I got to warn Eric and the others about this. Before it's too late!*

Chapter 13

One Who Cried Wolf

Okay that's enough of that. I don't want you to get spoiled by the ending. But now that you know her side of the story, here's mine. With Renée's mind just set on being away from me and the group, it was up to me and me alone to be the glue to hold the wings of this beaten white dove together and it worked at the beginning. Like volunteering at a local church where they even gave us a little money out of the kindness of their heart for our good and honest work. Right when things were finally looking good for us is when tragedy struck. We were at another diner eating because I don't want to celebrate at Bubba's Cafe for obvious reasons.

To our unpleasant surprise, Marcus and his gang found us even though we had been laying low for a while. Me, Delilah, Dom and the gang were sitting in a booth celebrating when all of a sudden a brick was thrown through our window. Delilah screamed in fright, waitresses, and the other staff members ducked to find cover. As if it were in slow motion I saw four guys in black ski masks bursting through the front door. I thought they were here to rob the place but no they were only here for us. They menacingly came towards our table but I was ready. With the advantage of surprise I tackled the leader and started to pummel him. The Twins and the rest of our group took over handling the rest. We beat them pretty good. They tried to flee but I managed to pull off one of the perps masks and to no one's surprise it was Marcus. He looked at me, snatched his mask back and ran off like the coward he is.

After that, we decided as a group to lay low once more, so the next day we were at headquarters, that is at my apartment; "I found that out back when the rest of our club were there for me when Renèe and I had that big fight." We all were scratching our heads trying to figure out a plan to combat Marcus and his goons as we heard about a big party happening on Saturday which is only two days away.

All of a sudden, we heard loud banging coming from the front door. Whoever was at the door was banging like a maniac. I walked over to the peephole as I figured it was one of Eric and Renèe's hippie neighbors who just ate too much grass if you know what I mean but I was surprised when I looked through that peephole to see Renèe all decked out.

I had to rub my eyes to make sure I wasn't dreaming. With zero hesitation, I opened the door and she rushed in and sat on the couch startling everyone. She was all out of breath, so the rest of us just waited for her to start talking. When she finally calmed down, she belted out how sorry she was about bursting in but she really needed our help.

"Why should we trust you? You're the one that left all of us in the dust, remember." Delilah said, giving her an evil glare. While others started to talk and argue among themselves. I had to be the one to hush them by sticking my hand out and waiting for them to all go silent.

"Let's hear her out first, then we'll decide what to do. Agreed?" They all said "Yes." in unison.

"Thank you, Eric. I knew I could count on you. I just came here to ask for help by doing me a huge favor ."

"HELP!" shrieked Delilah "What good—"

"Let the woman finish speaking Delilah." I interrupted mid shout while Delilah pouted. Not buying her pleas for help is one thing but I assumed she was here to rub it in our faces or maybe even bail Marcus out of jail since he "was" a close personal friend to us. But no, in fact it was something I didn't expect. I was startled when Renée said

"Thank you. It's Marcus…he has done or is going to do something really really bad."

"How bad Renée?"

"Remember the Brainiac and one hell of an engineer Huan Su Ming and a couple of other engineering students that suddenly disappeared two weeks ago."

"Yeah. What about it?" one of the group members had asked.

"Well, Marcus has kept them hostage in an abandoned warehouse all this time with their guns pointing at them. I took some photos of them among others and what he is currently planning and building is scary." She then spreads out these photos on the big wooden desk. We all took turns sitting at the couch passing the photographs around. I couldn't believe what I was seeing. It seems like our "friend" Marcus seemed like he was going to start a CIVIL WAR or a "Revolution" as he called it. He and his cronies already have AK-47s with other illegal weapons, not to mention he is keeping people hostage, that and he appears to be building

" **A BOMB ! ! !** " I exclaimed. Looking at the blueprint of what appears to be a homemade bomb.

Okay Marcus has gone too far…he has to be stopped. Renée then says "Yes. A bomb. He already has one done already but is making two more.I've already risked my life to get these photos." *So that's what he meant by a big party.* I thought to myself while Renée was busy waving the photos at our faces. She put them back down and said "Now you see why I came to you guys. We have to stop him."

"What do ya mean by we? Show this to the police…let them handle it." said Dom.

"The Police? Oh now we want bloodshed. This is our only chance to be the REAL HEROES."

"Renée." I said, trying to persuade her. "Dom is right. The police should be the ones to handle this. It's too dangerous for us to handle alone. We could all die."

" If Elijah were here with us right now, would he risk his life if it meant saving the city if not the world?"

" He would." I answered. "But that doesn't mean we have to be reckless. We can still stop Marcus without putting ourselves in danger. Besides I bet you don't even have a plan" crossing my arms.

"MY PLAN IS SIMPLE. We just sneak right in by an open window, find and grab the plans that's in his office, sneak right out and hand it over to the police and we'll be home free. That's it."

"That's it?! That's your amazing plan!" I exclaimed "We just waltz right in and——"

"Nooo…Sneak" Renèe clarified.

"Okay." I sighed. "So we sneak in, pray to dear GOD they don't catch us, find and grab the blueprint for the bomb that's somewhere in his office, and sneak right out to then hand it over to the police?! You're crazy, it will never work."

"Well, I don't see you coming up with any ideas." She pouted, her arms crossed and impatiently tapping her foot "Do yuh even have one? If so, I would love to hear 'em."

"Not at this minute but I'm sure if you gave me some time I—"

"We are not wasting any more time when lives are at stake." She replied, sharply. She then faced the remaining members of our group and yelled "Anyone else other than my future hubby got any bright ideas?" Of course her response made everyone reconsider theirs as the people around us said

"Nope."

"I'm good."

"I love your idea Renée."

"Good, so it's settled. We are going with mine."

She then took out a big roll of paper and unrolled it onto the table then headed over to the Victrola to put a record on for some background music which was Fortunate Son by Creedence Clearwater Revival. I cringed while hearing that. She looked at me funny and asked "What? " I gave her the same look back and muttered "Nothing." We then spent the next hour bickering while strategizing the plan. Where I was somehow successful in being able to convince Renée that we use the police as a last resort and allow some time to reason with Marcus to end his Tyranny before they handle it and she surprisingly agreed with me.

Chapter 14

Party Crashers

So it was settled, without a moment to lose we all piled into my van and drove to the police station. Once inside we demanded to meet with the chief of police. They were leary and a bit hostile toward us. But we were determined. The receptionist said, "We needed to fill out some forms and let them do some paperwork before speaking with him." We didn't like that one bit and I along with the others made such a racket stating "We can't do that now, lives are on the line here.", "We need the police chief down here now!", "It's a matter of life or death." and more. Being loud we got the attention of everyone in the lobby area, standing together as one. We were on the verge of being escorted out when we all decided to announce to everyone loud enough for all to hear "We know where a bomb is and won't tell anyone except the chief of police."

That did the trick, the chief of police in his bright dark blue uniform with bright brass buttons came rushing toward us. He pointed at me and Renée demanding "You two…come with me…now." Renèe and I followed him into his office. "You two better have some proof of your supposed bomb threat claims or else I'll have you arrested for Disturbing the Peace and Making a False Police Report." Renèe turned to look at me and smiled big. Without saying a word, she happily dumped the photos of the bomb, blueprint and the prisoners on his desk. The chief´s mouth just dropped. That room was so quiet, I swear you could've heard a pin drop. He quietly muttered

"What in the world?"

"Yeah, you heard us right. A bomb…that was right under your nose and you had no idea." Finishing my statement with an evil smirk. Renée jumped in to ask "Did that get your attention?" The chief nodded.

"Good. Now you listen to us old man on what we have to say. Or else you can do your own investigating when and where they would go off and by then it would be too late." I was surprised at Renée´s threat and muttered under my breath "Uhh what are you doing Renée?" To which she responded back by whispering in my ear to "Trust me, I know what I'm doin." I guess I had no other choice and backed off to let her have her moment.

I stepped aside and watched her grill the chief by bargaining that in exchange for this information, we get all the credit, be mentioned by the press of our good deeds and whatever charges our group has, should be dropped and wiped clean. When he refused, with an evil laugh Renée said "Okay, your loss but I wouldn't look at the paper tomorrow if I were you as your face is goin to be on the headlines for cheating on your wife by sleepin with your secretary."

Me and the chief were shocked. I whispered to her ear and asked "Is that true?" She whispered with a stern look back at me saying "I don´t know…maybe but what I am doing is called blackmailing honey. Look it up sometime." I guess that claim was apparently true as he stammered "How did yuh kn—uh-uh I mean…are you two blackmailing me?!"

"You're damn right we are!" I exclaimed going along with this set up, "So what's it gonna be chief, your good name tarnished or good coverage and praise for us by your police force for our cooperation on stopping the real villain."

The police chief murmured to himself before reluctantly agreeing with us that he'll make sure we get all the credit and praise by them and the school. We smiled in satisfaction, but it didn't last for long as he wanted to know where Marcus and the prisoners were located. She gave him an exact location where he immediately ordered all units to that location immediately, even the bomb squad. He then thanked us for our time but before shoving us out the door Renée looking worried asked

"What's going to happen to our friend Marcus?"

The answer he gave, wasn't the one she was looking for as with an evil chuckle had told her

"Let's just say when we are through with him, you won't be hearing from your "friend" for a long long time."

"Oh no you're not." I jumped in to argue "Renèe did the dirty work and even risked her life for these photos. The least you can do is call all your units to stand by for now and let us handle it and if things go bad for let's say an hour then you by all means go ahead and take him out." I paused and gulped as what I said wasn't easy to blurt out "Give us a chance." I coughed to ease my nerves and asked "What's it gonna be Chief? Your reputation or helping us save innocent people?"

He crossed his arms and grumbled to himself before telling us "Saving the innocent of course. You two got yourselves the hour headstart and it starts the moment you two leave my office." He then paused to lick his lips and added "Once we have Marcus, we will persuade the judge and the Supreme court of Louisiana to drop all charges on ya´ll." As we turned to leave he stopped us once again by whistling at us to "Grab these. If he is as dangerous as you says he is. Take them pistols.**YOU MAY FIND YOURSELF IN A WILD WEST SITUATION OUT THERE.** Now get outta my sight."

We did as instructed and took the two police issued pistols but not before hi-fiving each other on our way out of his office. We regrouped with our little band of righteous misfits and headed out to my van, cautiously drove to the warehouse and parked where the "Flying Monkey Committee" wouldn´t spot it.

We spread the map on the floor of my van and discussed what each of our roles were and where we would be heading. Our current plan was having The Irish Twins and the girls except for Delilah; who would be our lookout gal and warn us just in case Marcus and his gang come back. While the twins were assigned to distract them; Dom, Randy, Renée and I will sneak into the building hopefully undetected.

Once inside, we split up into two groups to cover more ground as just by looking at the blue abandoned warehouse seemed pretty big. Randy and Dom will free the prisoners with the key that Renée gave them while she and I go upstairs to Marcus' office, steal the blueprint and meet them by the open window where we came in. Once the blueprint has safely been turned over to the police, Renée and I then go back with weapons drawn, thanks to the police chief and persuade Marcus to give himself up.

Everything seemed to work as we planned, the Irish twins made a fool of themselves and got their attention, the goons chased after them and into their retrospective vehicles just as we planned. The twins got into my van and sped away with Marcus' group chasing after them. But what we weren't planning on were the guards still stationed at the door. Renée had to distract them when us "chickens" as she called us were too scared to confront them. To be fair, they each had AK47s strapped on their back and I had one lousy pistol with zero experience in how to shoot and reload the thing. Talk about a disadvantage. Renée distracted and led one of the guards away just enough for me and the boys to rush the remaining guard, disarm him, and neutralize him.

When the other guard turned his head back and noticed his buddy was gone, Renée took the advantage and knocked him out. Thanks to Eric's football strength and help with the others, Randy and I dragged the huskier one while Dom carried the other and Renée helped by holding the door open. From there we saw with our own eyes just how evil Marcus had fallen. Before us was misery and agony worse than Renée had described. We announced to the prisoners that we were here to rescue them and to quietly follow Randy and Dom out. Huan Su Ming helped us hustle all the prisoners out.

Following the last prisoner, we closed and locked the door, leaving the guards inside. Renée and I stood by the stairs watching the men make a break for it and once they did, we knew that was our cue to get moving. We headed upstairs but to our shock the office door was locked. I wanted to kick the door open but Renée stopped me saying "Relax, I can pick it." She then grabbed a hairpin from her pocket and proceeded to slowly pick the lock on the door. Hearing the clicking sound, I knew we were in. Swinging the door open, we went to work.

Searching frantically for the blueprint when suddenly, I heard Renée's joyous screech "I FOUND IT!" We unrolled the blueprint and saw that it was a device that appeared to be remotely activated with a design layout on what the bombs should look like too. Just as we were hi-fiving we heard a loud voice say "FUCK! THEY

WERE HERE!" I recognized that voice and it was Marcus. He had come back early. *Shit it's too soon.*

I peeked out the front door and saw Delilah trying desperately to get our attention by saying "Come on, Come on let's go they are almost here. I told her to go save herself, we'll find another way out. I closed the door and told Renée that Marcus and his goons came back too early, we gotta hide now. The only hiding spot was the closet but it was just big enough for one of us to fit in. I sighed as I knew what I had to do and just as she opened the door to the closet for one more try I pushed her in there with the blueprint in her hand and told her "I'm sorry" The moment I did said that, Marcus kicked the door open and immediately ordered me to "Turn around and drop the gun. If yuh know what's good for yuh." I heard them cock their guns, I slowly did as instructed. One of the goons that we knocked out earlier put my hands behind my back then everything faded to black.

The next thing I remember is feeling cold water splashed on me and I hear a loud booming voice shout "WHERE IS MY BLUEPRINT?!" Everything was still blurry but I remember being seated in a wooden chair and I couldn't see my arms so they were behind my back I guess.As my vision was beginning to focus, I realized that the booming voice sounded exactly like Marcus and since no one was sitting next to me that means that Renée hasn't been found yet so with that I answered

"Your Blueprint to What? Your BRAIN. I think you lost that...a long time ago." with a toothy grin. I wasn't smiling for long as suddenly I saw his hand make a fist and like slow motion, watched in horror as he made contact to the left side of my face and kicked my chair where I was looking at the ceiling fan. Lifting my chair to face him menacingly said "Now that I have your full attention, where is it?"

"Where's what?"

"Don't you play dumb with me Eric Striker. I have been fooled once already by trustin Renée as why else would yuh be here? " He paused to stroke his beard and asked "If yuh don't have my plan to start my Revolution. Who does?!"

"Renée." I answered with a sigh. "She has your precious blueprint and is as far away from here as possible." as I looked down at the floor. Marcus lifted my head up and looked me in the eyes to see if I was telling the truth…I guess. Marcus is dumber than I thought as he bought it and said "Well she couldn't have gotten far." He then whistled at the two bodyguards and said "Let's move." As he got up, one of the guards handed him a strange looking object and he turned some sort of clock and I heard ticking. He then placed it at my feet and before leaving said "Congratulations Eric, you're our new test dummy. Better Pray to dear God that Huan Su Ming who made this, was a dud. I guess there is only one way to find out." (He laughs manically at my face:)

"Better hope your sweetheart comes back in time to save you. You only got 15 minutes of life left…but she doesn't know that." I remember their evil looks as they left to go search for Renée.

Chapter 15

Mr. Damsel In Distress

There I was strapped to a wooden chair with a bomb underneath my seat. I never in a million years thought things would end up like this but here we are. When the coast was clear as I didn't hear them anymore, Renée came out of the closet. With tears running down her face she kept saying how this was all her fault and promising to get us out of this. She tried pulling on the rope that strapped me to the chair but that didn't work. It was tied too tight. Minutes seemed to fly by and the ticking clock showed I only had ELEVEN minutes left.... TO LIVE.

My whole concern was to get her to safety. I told her "We can't waste any more time. Marcus and the boys could be back here any minute. GET OUT OF HERE RENÉE. I'll get out of this somehow and meet you outside. Now Go! Get Outta here!!"

"I am not leaving you Eric!" she sobbed. "We came to this warehouse together and we are leavin together. I am getting you out of this damn rope or we'll die trying." I tried to reason with her. "Renée, your mother already lost one child. I won't let her lose another one, now go. I'll get out of this and I'll meet you outside I promise."

She looked at me and nodded slowly saying "I'll be waiting for you outside." wrapping her arms around me, we kissed deeply and she turned away to run out the door. Alone, I thought *I am no James Bond or Macgyver.* Marcus had taken my gun and placed it on the desk. *Is this how it's going to end for me?* I thought. *Well if I do end up dying at least I'll go down in a blaze of glory like I always wanted. With nothing else to lose I prayed to dear god or the fog if it's still out there somewhere listening to send someone to help me get out of here in one piece.*

Just as I closed my eyes trying to come to grips with my fate, I heard a faint voice that sounded like a drill sergeant's saying "I got you soldier." Opening my eyes and in front of me was this tall black man in full dress military uniform. Strangely his name tag plate was blank. I have no idea who this person was.

But I prayed he was here to rescue me. I watched in pure amazement as he quickly reached in his front left pocket, pulling out an army knife and walked closer to me. I felt the rope around my hands drop away and I was free. I blurted out "Thank you" and realized that there was something off about "my hero". He seemed to be glowing. Like there was a flame or some kind of light surrounding him. I just chalked it up to it being a trick of the light in the office space.

Regardless, I was free and I got up asking him "Who are you and how did you—" He stopped me and said "Call me E. I was around the neighborhood when I heard you call for help. Got this knife from my time in the army." as I saw him putting his knife in his back pocket. "Save your questions till we are out of this, okay." I didn't have the strength to walk out on my own since Marcus had beaten me pretty good, he put his arm around me and we walked out the door together.

We had gotten out just in the nick of time. We heard the bomb explode back in the room and a fireball blew open the door and was now starting to spread. The fire got out of control fast as black smoke and fog quickly covered the hallway. The heat was so intense that it was hard to even breathe. It felt like the skin of my face was burning. If it weren't for this stranger E guiding me to safety, I would have been a goner. Once we got to the steps and started to slowly head down the six flights, the man asked "So you got a name stranger or do I have to guess?"

"Eric. Eric Striker is my name." I answered

He surprised me as he stopped to look me up and down and said calmly

"You're not him. You're blonde and dress like him but you look nothin like the man. Who are you?"

I didn't know if I should tell this stranger the truth or not but I did anyway against my better judgment.

"You're right, I'm not him. Call me crazy but my real name is Lucas Robinson and uhh Imma Time-Traveler from the year

2022 and I am helping people like Eric and his fiancé Renée I guess."

"Time Traveler?" he questioned doubtfully. "What brought you all the way out here?" He asked.

"A Mysterious Green Fog." I answered

"Really?" E had asked bewildered. He shook his head and asked a very interesting and personal question which I guess was to change the subject "You got a wife and kids? Lucas. "

"I'm not ready for all that yet, E. I'm only 20 years old." I said with a faint smile. "I got a girlfriend though, her name is Emily but what about you? Got a wife? Kids? "

"I never really had the time fo—" he stopped as we both heard and saw the flames getting bigger and closer to us as they started to reach the 4th level while we just made it on the 2nd level.

"We better get moving." I said as I finally had enough strength to walk on my own. When we got to the front door,it was stuck. As the flames got closer to me, he said "We push on three and dive… ready!" I nodded. We counted together and pushed, I felt the flames come barreling towards us and that my friends was the moment we both dived and landed hard on the rocky pavement outside.

I tried to get up but I only had enough strength to look ahead and see Renée along with firefighters and paramedics starting to run towards me. I looked to the left and saw E still on the ground. I tried reaching out to him but everything faded to black.

When I came to. I was lying on a gurney inside an ambulance while the paramedics did some testing. I panicked and immediately asked

"Where is he?"

"Who?" Asked Renée along with the other paramedics.

"The man who saved me."

To my shock, Renée looking concerned said "Eric, honey, everyone has been accounted for. The only person who was in that building was you and only you. No one saved you."

"But there was a man, he was laying on the ground right next to me. I saw him with my own eyes." I took a couple of deep breaths in and out and added

"You–You must've missed him."

"Eric, calm down. You just imagined this man rescuing you. The smoke was poisoning your brain, you were the only person on the ground that we saw."

"No, he was there. I saw him, clear as day."

"What did this man look like, kid?" one of the paramedics chimed in to ask. I gave them the description of the army man where everyone looked at me crazy while one of the paramedics volunteered himself to go check. The moment one of the guys left,

Renée was stunned, her eyes and mouth widened. She took a few seconds to compose herself and asking again she said

"What did you say this man looked like?"

I described again what I saw, with trembling hands she withdrew a photo from her purse asking

"Is this him?"

I leaned in closer to take a better look and it was the same man that I saw in the picture wearing the exact same uniform.

"That's him!" I exclaimed. "Who is he?".

Renée looking stunned answered

"Eric, the man or E that you called him is none other than my brother Elijah. He has been dead for over a month now." She went on to explain that I was there at his funeral but I just kind of tuned her out. I couldn´t believe that I-I-I was saved by a ghost or rather some guardian angel of sorts. I mean it couldn't have been anyone else as everyone left. I know what I saw. Maybe it was my or Eric´s head messing me with the stress of you know not dying, that saved me not myself. You gotta believe me, don´t you?

Do you find it strange that there was this flame behind E. too and the rope that just somehow came undone when he freed me with the army knife. Now that I think of it, I don´t remember even seeing any cut marks on the rope..

"Oh my god." Renée said, covering her mouth interrupting my thoughts in shock. She took her hand off her mouth and continued saying "Eric. My prayers were answered. I prayed that he would protect you and guide you out of there and he did just that." Looking up to the sky she blew kisses shouting "Thank you, Thank you, Elijah." Suddenly the paramedic came back and said "There was no man there. The only thing I found was this. Is this yours?" as he showed me the same army knife that E or Ellijah used to get me free. Renée was shocked as she asked

"That's not Eric's knife. Eric never owned or used a knife like that before. Where did you find it?"

"It was just a couple feet from where we got Eric actually. Don't know how we missed it the first time. Maybe this stranger really was here."

After getting checked out at the hospital, the police told me that the combat knife the paramedics found had the initials "E.B." carved on the handle. "E.B." Wow! E.B. The only E.B. it could have been "Elijah....Bowman."

Chapter 16

From Beyond The Grave

Marcus and his goons may have been arrested and kicked out of the university for good but I didn't want to leave this time period or Renée alone just yet and I think the mysterious fog knew it too.....at least I hope it did. More than anything else I needed to pay my respects to my hero...Elijah Bowman. I had to. I owe him my life. Without him, Eric and I wouldn't be alive today and that means I wouldn't be speaking with you all today.

The very next day I told Renée my plan and we agreed on going to the grave together.. I dressed in all black for this occasion while Renée on the other hand decided to wear the exact opposite. She wore a bright black and yellow polka dot dress. In my mind, you don't usually wear bright colors to a cemetery but Renée clarified that she is only dressing like this because Polka dots and the color yellow were Ellijah's favorite. Since I've never been there before, she directed me to the cemetery. Holding hands, we walked through the cemetery grounds. Abruptly she stopped and announced "This is it."

I looked at the Cross Marble Tombstone where Elijah Bowman's full name, Date of birth Death, and rank were listed. Renée told me that he was gonna be buried at Arlington National Cemetery in DC but her family disagreed and requested that he be buried here in New Orleans. As we stood in front of the grave, Renée told me how he had been awarded a Silver Star and Purple heart. I was right on how he was in fact a combat medic. He had served in the 5th Medical Battalion, 4th Infantry Division. According to Renée he died a hero as she in tears described how the Army Officers who knocked on their door told them the story of how he died. According to them they were in the midst of some battle. (The battle she is referring to is known to us as the Cambodian Campaign.) He had just put the last wounded man in the helicopter.as it was taking off, he got shot in the chest. He was initially rescued but sadly succumbed to his injury a day later on July 23rd 1970. He died a week shy of his 26th birthday which according to his tombstone was August 1st, 1944.

Amidst her storytelling, Renée stopped to say "Hi brotha." with tears running down her face gave his tombstone a good bear hug. I heard her whisper "Hope Gramps is keepin yuh busy up there. Not a day goes by that I don't think of yuh." She then broke down and cried. When I was patting her shoulder trying to console her, something very strange happened.

I heard a voice whisper in my ear saying "Thanks for all your help, Lucas. I can take it from here." I felt a jolt and a rush of cold air right through me. Turning around I heard a whistle.

That's when I saw a ball of light floating near an old weeping willow tree a few feet away from us. The ball of light changed its shape and definition, I saw it become the figure of the Elijah Bowman who had saved me. Renée didn't appear to see him as she continued to cry at the foot of Elijah's grave. To my amazement I watched him slowly raise his left hand in an army salute. I smiled and returned the salute. He returned with a bright pearly white smile.

We stared at each for what seemed like an eternity but was probably only for a few seconds. Then I watched Elijah slowly put his hand down and assume the military "At Ease position." Call me crazy but I watched the man nod his head as he slowly faded starting with his legs then his chest where he eventually dissolved into thin air.

I rubbed my eyes as I couldn't believe what I had just seen. As I was rubbing them, my elbow banged on something hard. Turning my head and opening my eyes, I saw the thing I hit was a window with the green fog in the background. To my amazement it was the window to my 2014 red Chevy Impala and I was now seated behind the steering wheel. I guess the fog isn't done with me as I am still staring into the dark green fog.

Wherever I end up next better somewhere nice and warm with zero horsin around. I mean it this time. But if I know the fog, I will be in for a big surprise.

........TO BE CONTINUED.......